FOR LORENZO'S BLEAK AUDIENCE IN THE WALL

About the Sources

The author would like to say something about his character. He's not an educated man and his cultural choices are uncritical and superficial. He belongs to nowadays; the web gives him almost all the bricks he builds his odd world with. And the web, you know, is full of broken bricks (or mistakes, if you prefer).

About the Language

Each book is a complete world, with its own laws. And it often speaks one language only. Here all the characters – Italian, French, English – speak today's English. Sometimes French and Italian words emerge to give a touch of cultural colour – to make a particular atmosphere. After all, the real world speaks English – the Latin of nowadays, as you know.

The author is an Italian poet who wrote this novella directly in English. He describes himself as *a Turinese writer who writes in English*. This is not a one-off experiment – he simply felt that it was better to be a storyteller through this medium. This is the beginning – he hopes – of a marvellous (if slightly strange) adventure.

FELLINESQUE

A NOVELLA BY
ANDREA BIANCHI

Published by Cinnamon Press,
Meirion House,
Tanygrisiau,
Blaenau Ffestiniog,
Gwynedd LL41 3SU
www.cinnamonpress.com

The right of Andrea Bianchi to be identified as author of this work
has been asserted by him in accordance with the Copyright,
Designs and Patent Act, 1988. © 2013 Andrea Bianchi.
ISBN 978-1-907090-87-5
Designed and typeset in Garamond by Cinnamon Press. Cover
design by Cottia Fortune-Wood © Cottia Fortune-Wood.
Cinnamon Press is represented by Inpress and by the Welsh Books
Council in Wales. The publisher acknowledges the support of the
Welsh Books Council Printed in Poland
Fellinesque is a work of fiction. Any resemblance to any person is
entirely co-incidental.

Acknowledgements

The author's thanks are due to Harri Pritchard Jones (his father
in literature), to Jan Fortune (his brave publisher), to Silvana
Siviero (his beloved wife), who have made this publication
possible with their precious advice.

The author wishes to express his gratitude also to Dafydd Prys
Ap Morus for publishing three chapters from *Fellinesque* in his
literary magazine *Blue Tattoo* (Issues 3, 5, 9).

CONTENTS

FOREWORD

When you see or read of characters in an inter-active relationship with their author, one immediately thinks of the works of Pirandello. And *Fellinesque* owes a great deal to his perceptions of reality. Indeed, Andrea Bianchi is a compatriot of the Italian dramatist.

Bianchi is a poet, novelist and translator from Turin. The work was composed in English, but it ranges through many languages and cultures in an exciting way; and through different ages as well.

As we know, works of literature owe a deal, but not everything, to their author. There is another partner in the process, namely the medium used, the matrix of the actions and characters in the work. In the body of this work there are acknowledgements to the way memories and supposed memories, personal and archetypal and suppressed, contribute to the fiction. David Jones called these the gratuitous element in the process of writing.

Lest I make this work sound like a treatise, let me emphasise that it is a fascinating read, and the colourful panoramas we are offered are as attractively bizarre as an Ionesco play. We have numerous dialogues between the author-protagonist and Professor Cavallo, an *alter ego*. But we also rove through Revolutionary France, where we admire the deep research Andrea Bianchi has carried out. There is a wealth of interesting narrative within the web of explorations of the relationship between different concepts of reality.

Here is an example of the dialogue between the author and Professor Cavallo, which illustrates the point:

'... I think I had better make myself clear. I see that reality is ill with pretence; or rather, I saw it die of pretence... this morning. So I yearn for a genuinely false reality where I can feel real; a reality that is as true as it is clearly false. I want it for me but for you too, obviously. It is a game that I like and that we can play together, if you want. Listen. This morning I was in bed, lying on my side, and I was looking out at the cloudless sky through the French window. Then the first swallow dived down drawing a diagonal in the light blue rectangle; then the second one, in the same way. That quick sequence of flights hurt me. In the past it would have invited me to write something, a line, a sentence; this morning I didn't feel that delight, and what I saw seemed out of place, wrong. The second swallow was particularly deceptive.'

'You want to build a reality ex novo. Don't you commit the sin of conceitedness?'

'Well, isn't it what we all do when we interpret reality and more so when we envisage writing about it?'

The book steers clear of being a formal discussion of the nature of reality, at the same time as it introduces the ideas of the French philosopher, Jean Baudrillard, author of the seminal work, *Simulacra and Simulation,* which has been so influential on Andrea Bianchi's vision of the nature of life.

These works, by Baudrillard, Pirandello, Fellini and others, raise the question of the author as a god figure. This work reminds me of the old concept of Divine Providence as being an author who also takes part in the staging of his work, as a sort of actor-manager, responding and adapting as the created characters and situations react with suggestions he has to respond to.

Fellinesque is challenging but very rewarding, and a pleasure to read.

Harri Pritchard Jones

THIS BOOK IS FOR SILVANA,
THE WISE AND BELOVED BRICK TO WHICH
I AM TIED LIKE A YELLOW BALLOON.

BUT IT IS ALSO FOR HARRI PRITCHARD JONES,
BECAUSE IF THIS WERE A DEGREE THESIS,
NO DOUBT HARRI WOULD HAVE BEEN
MY SUPERVISOR.

FELLINESQUE

1

HERE IS THE PROFESSOR

The characters mustn't seem to be ghosts, but they must be creatures, immutable beings from the imagination; so they will be more real and solid than the actors' fickle naturalness.

Luigi Pirandello
Six Characters in Search of an Author

I think: he is coming with a book under his arm and my trap will snap shut on me and I won't be able to do anything about it because I can't control what I am creating. Let's begin like this. I see the evening arriving as I sit at the bar where we have our appointment. The wide square, the river, the hill, all is bright. Shortly, Professor Egisto Cavallo will come, as I have decided; he will cross the square with his walking stick and his book. I don't know if anybody will accompany him: no, alone is better, much better. So I scan the edges of the vast rectangle, the riverside flanked with lit streetlamps, the various and hurried people walking and the river of cars and lorries, tramways and buses, out of which the old journalist – and retired teacher, writer, art critic, the man that met Hemingway and Picasso and other giants – will suddenly appear ... Here comes this old man, a stooping figure, walking stick and broad-brimmed hat, out from the movement and the noise, almost closed in a bubble of silence, framed like an image from the past.

'Oh, good evening, Professor. Please, sit down. Would you like something to drink?'

'No, thank you. I'm in a hurry. I would like Coralba to have this book straight away. Dear Lorenzo, it was very kind of you to offer to drive me to Coralba's.'

'No, don't thank me, Professor. This is not altruism. All I need is a story – that alas will be neither simple nor clear – and you are giving me this by your presence here. I would say: with your *existence* here. I want a skeleton of simple actions that takes *my-need-to-speak* somewhere.'

'You look worried, my friend. Is it for the book you are working on? You know that I appreciated your poems and I want to help you.'

'Thank you very much, Professor. But I did not doubt it. I think I had better make myself clear. I see that reality is ill with pretence; or rather, I saw it die of pretence… this morning. So I yearn for a genuinely false reality where I can feel real; a reality that is as true as it is clearly false. I want it for me but for you too, obviously. It is a game that I like and that we can play together, if you want. Listen. This morning I was in bed, lying on my side, and I was looking out at the cloudless sky through the French window. Then the first swallow dived down drawing a diagonal in the light blue rectangle; then the second one, in the same way. That quick sequence of flights hurt me. In the past it would have invited me to write something, a line, a sentence; this morning I didn't feel that delight, and what I saw seemed out of place, wrong. The second swallow was particularly deceptive.'

'You want to build a reality *ex novo*. Don't you commit the sin of conceitedness?'

'Well, isn't it what we all do when we interpret reality and more so when we envisage writing about it?'

'No, it isn't so! Our case is different. I feel you force me to stay here, while I would like to be somewhere else, if I had the freedom to choose; at home, for example, among my books, my pictures. Instead *I want to go* to Coralba's; it is so: I realise that you desire what I desire. This is what I mean when I talk about conceitedness. You must consider yourself a sort of god, even if a minor one.'

'There is no other way, believe me. And I am like you: forced to act according to a will that is outside me. Today you will see me making a town with streets and squares, with a dirty river full of lights; hills surrounding it on one side, the mountains on the other. I will make a clear or grey sky, as you like it. And the

14

people will be smiling, they will fill every corner, street, avenue, square, on foot, by car, on motorcycles, tramways; they will not wish to look around or, on the contrary, they will not stop a moment to observe anything.'

'People? Strange! Your poetry, let's say, is an objective poetry of objects and inner rooms that keeps life out. I consider it interesting because it so closely resembles certain pictures that I love. Indeed, I don't think that people are your business, Lorenzo.'

'Not true people, maybe – those people that I can't bend to my desire – but your type that I can manipulate in part. From the mood of the almost-people, believe me, can depend the nature of the story I am writing. I would not like them to frown, for example, but to accompany me, always winking encouragement. Yet this desire of mine prevents me from continuing a story that would otherwise pour from me. Instead, I labour to think.'

'What do you mean?'

'I am the story, but I also depend on it in part. It writes me, detaching itself from me because it's stronger than me. And, besides, it denies me the big spaces, the empty ones or those consumed by the deletions that kill men and pull down houses. It is like a comic. Do you recall the comic page of *Mickey Mouse* faded by water or humidity? It is difficult to move in this nothing that is full of me. So many snares hamper my feeble fantasy preventing me from drawing the background. So the story continuously changes the rules of the game. Where I would like a house, it imposes a church; where I would expect a garden, a square appears. When I walk along a street wanting to see a woman, a man comes round the corner; when I would like to be an invisible man, someone calls me screaming among the silent houses.'

'What bizarre words, my young friend. But now please take me to Coralba's.'

As I drive, I realise that speaking tires me. Something breaking inside my mind (or soul, perhaps) and, consequently, the square opens a big white gash swallowing many things – houses, passers-by, a line of streetlights – and widening more and more. It doesn't matter: I take the opportunity to study the street guide. I never learned the names of the streets and the squares of Turin, my city. It is the model for the imaginary one I am building; but I keep it strange, foreshortening certain places to complete it. I've stopped my small car in a closed petrol station: I open the street guide on the wheel: 23-B4. Here is the big white rectangle near the light blue ribbon of the river. It is the biggest square; in the past it used to host Carnivals. Coralba lives in the hills, in a two-storey house near similar buildings encircled by a big park: so the professor said. I have a kind thought for him: to drive with care, to take care of his china fragility.

A little effort, and the white of the square becomes tinged with things and people again; a new pulp, a new juice making the beginning of this journey appealing. So, we go through the square, then cross the bridge, looking at the river, unable to resist the appeal of water – I control my emotions, my great enemy. People mustn't sense anything, mustn't sniff the truth. We sail the crowd as if we were on board a ship pushed by a gentle wind. But we are also a part of it, so nobody will guess that he is the creature, and I am the creator.

*

When we penetrate the fog, I wonder why I've made it so thick and hostile. The wet road suddenly becomes steep and curves in sharp bends, it seems to be in accord with a taste I didn't know I had, for self-punishment. The professor looks at me with his small semi-closed, almost blind eyes: I know what he is thinking because I think what he must think. But he has a margin of freedom and can change it as he likes. Now I find he was thinking that I am an inept.

'I don't know to what extent you are aware of your limits. Not even the road that we must cover is safe, and I don't think the rest of this odd adventure will be. I beg you to take me back to my occupations. I am not made for these things.'

'I would like to remain alone, but I can't. I must speak with someone. And then, mustn't you take that book to Coralba?'

'You're right, but you get on my nerves, so I forget my duties.'

'By the way, you didn't speak about it.'

'The book? I thought you recognized it. It is a collected poems. Your collected poems.'

'Incredible! *The Room Continues*. I didn't know Coralba loved poetry.'

But does Cora love poetry? And how long has she loved it for? Maybe, in a moment of distraction, I thought it had to be so. Who knows? I don't know myself; I can't expect to know Cora. "The characters mustn't seem to be ghosts, but they must be creatures, immutable beings from imagination; more real and solid than the actors' fickle naturalness." – Pirandello would say. From him I took the idea of playing 'let's pretend'; to duplicate, triplicate myself, and at the same time to move away these pieces of myself, making them in part

17

different from myself. All is born from literature; a unique, true world that is closed and perfect. I was born from Pirandello, from his work, he is my father and mother; he hatched me among the pages (or on the stages) of his *Six Characters*, and I came to life, that is to literature, theatre: then I slid inside other books, other theatres. Maybe I am a being of his imagination. Who knows?

2

WHERE IS CORA?

How much of a house's expression is within what surrounds it!

Ferruccio Busoni
Thoughts About Expression in Architecture

Professor Egisto Cavallo was the first to rebel.

It's now impossible to persuade him to put his hands down on the old worm-eaten table as I think he should. Evelina, Coralba's mother, a sprightly ninety-year-old, is a fragile woman without hands! I didn't manage to model them resting on the keyboard of that improbable upright piano that lacks one lateral side. I will consider completing her later, and then the piano. I am listening to her fragile voice and looking at her diaphanous face, that could decay leaving the skull... smiling. Where is Coralba? Will she enter this room, which is a terrible mess, from the corridor that leads to two other rooms? It is only a store-room of old things where thousands of layers of dust pile up like ancient boredom, or pain, or joy maybe; it makes no difference.

'When Stravinsky shook hands with me, I was so excited. *The Rite of Spring*: how wonderful! And he, such a charming man...'

'Sure,' the professor says, as if talking to himself, 'sure, but I prefer Schoenberg. The Russian is all glitters and rhythm, he is a body without soul; instead the Austrian looks inside himself, he manages to read himself deeply... or Busoni, the one who said: "How much of a house's expression is within what surrounds it!".'

A stretch of path is framed by the window, the one opposite the door; the path window. In the corner where the women do the cooking, there is another window overlooking a scant piece of meadow with three bent trees. The vast park includes many two or three-storey buildings like this house; they are similar to mountain houses, with their large grey stone roofs. They are like a medieval village, and so they have their castle; a big manor that I wouldn't call a villa; it is more like a small abandoned factory. It is Carlone's villa, the publisher's. And it is where the lords of the small village live. For thirty years there has been an old black locomotive on a rusty segment of railway; it doesn't arrive from or depart to anywhere, it is immovable, or it moves but on a metaphysic journey.

Well, it's a clever construction. I'm proud of that. But all these trees and meadows and houses make me busy to the point that I haven't been able to make Evelina's hands appear from the sleeves of her old rose blouse. They might move on the keyboard making a melody. This reveals one of my flaws, or qualities: I can always conclude the works I like, but I falter over simple problems if I don't like what causes them. Then I put them aside. For example, the old woman's hands would have been hidden by the piano, so I couldn't have seen them from here because the instrument to the right of the path window, obscures the hands. I can see only the piano's rear, similar to a drawerless bureau. So, why should I create the hands? You could object that I would hear them play. Yes, it's true. I have probably been lazy.

Cora should come in now. *But she doesn't.* I concentrate, but I feel strange, as though I am some sorcerer's apprentice. Come in, Cora! Come from the dark corridor. (It is also full of things.) Come here, dear! Appear at the door, please! *But she doesn't.* I feel the eyes of the two old people on me. I lift my head. They look at me with the staring eyes of wax dolls; or, maybe, with scornful smiles on their faces.

'Where is Cora?' I say in a strange voice.

'I don't know,' answers Evelina like a doll, a very old doll.

'Dear Lorenzo, you keep disappointing me. You should have made sure Coralba was at home waiting for us,' the professor says in his professorial tone.

Beyond this wall there are other walls and many things and much dust, and Cora's small awkward shape should be born there with its cardigan and woollen caps and half gloves... wool from thousands of badly mixed colours... And it should look like an old nun with a baby face and red cheeks. It should. *But it doesn't.* Is this another rebellious act?

Just so, three mischievous characters. I don't expect blind obedience, but I want a modicum of collaboration. Instead Cora doesn't appear, and the two old people have disappeared now, or rather, some parts remain: a leg, an arm, half a face suspended near the sink where one of them was, a limb behind the piano where the other was. I think about what to do, and the sham world created by my fantasy crumbles around me, leaving me in a quiet white space; the trees faded too, and the village, but not the engine.

There it is... moving. It suddenly speeds up, then slowly stops in what is pure white snow, or in a strange thing shining white like snow. I don't understand at all. Colours and masses are filling up this hollow bit by bit; they are defining its edges and swelling its inside with figures and things and a dense warm life from long ago, perhaps the twenties. Noises are forming at last; the train announcing its arrival at the station.

It is appearing in relief on a glossy, shimmering background; the black shield of a knight, or a black hatch in front of me, so near that I'm not able to recognise it as the dusty front of the engine. I think others are creating this vision, this past that I can't know and can't create. They must have put me into their dreams.

All around the sky is white with sun and sultriness. It's warm, even hot, because it is July. I'm looking at the crowd wiping sweat from their faces, the ladies fanning themselves with their papers or brochures; someone has a fan adorned with flowers or figures, or strange shapes I can't distinguish. I feel the bodies around me, the physical contact with them; one pushes me, and the shove projects me... inside: I am a part of my creation again, again a character in my dream. In two steps I reach the side of the train and see the long chimney with its grey smoke, the expression of the black, strong, iron body, which is sleeping, warmer than the hot air of the afternoon. There is a flimsy balcony with a peeling rail above the engine; it looks like a train belvedere. In fact it belongs to a seven-storey house, but strangely was added by me (or by others) to the railway station. There are some elegant people on it. There is a young woman.

I'm looking at the figures on the balcony: something impresses me, I look at them again and notice that girl's blousy bodice and square cut collar, her pearl necklace, her snowy skin whitened by lemon juice. Her smiling face... is someone I think I know. She is not wearing a hat and her eyes have a dark line. She is so beautiful. She looks like... Evelina. Three men stand close to her. The one on the right is a young man with pearl grey Oxford bags and a dark double-breasted jacket. On the left there are a gigolo in a white morning dress and a middle-aged man in a dark blue suit.

I didn't know I knew any of this. No, I can't correct it if I have made a mistake. I would like to be on that balcony and chat with that beauty, as the young fellow is doing. Look! They are laughing. Who knows what they

24

are thinking? I should know, but instead I am steering the course less and less, I am more and more a slave to it... And now someone is speaking in front of me: 'The good old days, my dear!'; 'In our days, dear Egisto.'; 'Oh yes, Evelina, yes, dear.'... The shiny balcony wavers in the afternoon light. I wouldn't like it to vanish; but the image yellows and is silent, the people are faceless, the heavy black train sheds white all around. It is the white of pain and it is slowly licking at things and people; swallowing them. Then it rises like a river in flood, rising white like lime...

3

ODD PARTY

A charming woman, Scrope Purvis thought her (knowing her as one does know people who live next door to one in Westminster), a touch of the bird about her, of the jay, blue-green, light, vivacious, though she was over fifty, and grown very white since her illness.

Virginia Woolf
Mrs Dalloway

What has just happened deserves proper investigation.

I must return to the past as soon as possible to clear this up. But first of all I must find a way to proceed. Meanwhile the room has become firm and I can walk around. The two old people have disappeared again. How strange. They spoke so kindly and quietly in that time fog earlier. How strange.

'Not so strange, dear,' a voice says.

Coralba is smiling at me from the piano.

'Oh, Cora, what a pleasant surprise. When did you arrive?'

'Now.'

'And your mother? And the professor?'

'They are having a short walk in the garden.'

'In the snow?'

It is snowing heavily outside. I run the risk of becoming crazy; it was spring before, now it is winter.

'What clothes are they wearing? Are they warm enough?'

'You are a strange creator,' Cora says.

'I may be. But there should be a way to put me and all of you in order. For example, where were you?'

'In your mind, I think... my Lord,' she says laughing.

I have a journey in my mind now; it will take place in the near future. I don't think they know anything about it yet.

'We should choose the best poems in your book if you want to make a good impression on that Welsh poet, the Bard, my dear.'

I am mistaken again.

'So, you know about the journey. Well. Maybe you know more than I do.'

She leafs through my book with intent eyes, before looking up at me, but she doesn't answer. Instead she begins to declaim:

I am tired,
the day is tired
and the light.
Thicker the colours
and more solid,
with few shades.
Monotonous the day
inviting you to sleep,
a sweet sleep.
You long to sleep
for a long time,
hoping for rain,
for the wind to break the heat.

'Wonderful, it is "August". Do you like it?' I say truly interested in her answer.

'Not particularly. I prefer "I Am a Corridor of Rain".'

'Why did you read it, then?'

'I don't know. Do you always know what you do?'

We sit facing each other at the table and I notice her likeable dumpiness. She has two piles of yellowish sheets with her. My poems, I think. She must have copied them. I wonder why.

'Are they my poems? Why did you ...?'

'Yes, they are. My things are written on light blue sheets,' she answers.

Now I remember that she has written four very long, unpublished novels and that Father Ballet (the editor at Carlone's Press) had appreciated one of them a little. What is the title? *A Touch of the Bird about Her*, yes, of course. She likes Virginia Woolf. Virginia is her model. But there is a problem: her rough copies are too rough; those she wrote by hand are illegible, whilst those she typed with that old typewriter of hers are full of corrections in ink. You might like to say some kind words about her work, but you would need to first understand what it is that she has written. "Dear", I told her some time ago, "your writing must be clear."

'I prefer to do it my own way. And as for copying your poems, it's the same thing – I prefer my own methods.'

'But Carlone's Press hasn't published anything of yours yet. Maybe I'm right, aren't I?' I say bitterly.

'Apropos of that,' says Cora, her cheeky face raised, 'can't you do anything to change Father Ballet's mind a little? You are the creator after all.'

A small white gash appears, cut by the knife of my impatience when I put a stop to that character and her disrespectful words. She is terrible... Suddenly I feel something in the air... Will it be a surprise? A good or a bad one? This world is mine... only in part. So everything is possible... even rebellion against me. As I look around things come back: colours and noises. These last are few because it is still snowing, softly and white. Many flowerpots full of flowers appear here and there. The room decorates itself with cheerful festoons. The table has returned with its tasty army of steaming plates. And people are speaking happily: people I don't know.

Maybe... Maybe I know them, like my own blood. Here are their files:

Name: Palandro; profession: writer; character: very serious, maybe too serious; appearance: average height, thin, sober and elegant, someone a woman can consider charming.

Name: The Girl Who Wants To Paint A Masterpiece; profession: waitress; character: always cheerful, maybe too cheerful; appearance: every man would prefer the good steak with potatoes that she is able to serve.

Name: Schoolmistress; profession: schoolmistress; character: a fat and bumptious schoolmistress; appearance: terribly fat, like Gertrude Stein in the famous photo with Alice Toklas.

Name: Michele; profession: slave-poet; character: calm, submissive and mute; appearance: a middle-aged man in a dark blue suit.

Name: nameless people; profession: none: character: frenzied and noisy; appearance: incomplete, sometimes without arms and legs, heads or other parts of their bodies.

Well. Now I have all the elements to make a good painting of the party. There are three groups against the confusion made by the partial people and their parts. Cora is talking with me about her friend, The Girl Who Wants To Paint A Masterpiece, who is also present. Schoolmistress is conversing with Evelina, who has returned from her walk, and a middle-aged man is mute in her shade. Finally Professor Cavallo, who has also returned, and Palandro are discussing Jean Baudrillard and his theories; there is a neutral character without arms with them. It is a beautiful summer day outside.

Well, this party is rippling around me with its arms and legs and laughing faces. I see three islands made of whole and firm bodies; I belong to one of them. The people in these islands speak clearly against a flurry of meaningless words from the sea of fragmented bodies.

'Look at this, and this, and this,' Cora says, showing me a few large sheets painted with strange watercolours.

She emphatically declares: 'She has an enormous talent, hasn't she?'

'I'm sorry, I have no talent for evaluating things of art. But the colours are very nice, so cheerful and delicate,' I answer with an idiotic smile on my face.

The waitress has the same idiotic face as mine while she is looking at Cora. She is observing Cora's lips as they move. She is stunned. This is a marvellous place where everything is possible, very far from the stinking kitchen and rough people she serves every day. Here, the chrysalis-waitress becomes a butterfly-paintress (excuse me for my trite metaphor). A nice fairy-tale: but she is like a statue and mute as a statue. It's a pity.

Besides us Schoolmistress is speaking to Evelina about the slave-poet – that quiet middle-aged man in a dark blue suit. Schoolmistress is enormous and aggressive; Evelina is thin and thinking of other things, maybe of her youth. No, I am sure: her thoughts are about her youth. I should know something about my creatures, as I am continuously saying. Maybe I am a second-hand god, but I am doing a similar job – as you are continuously thinking. But it's true: fundamental things must be reiterated, as at school when you learn something. You are my audience in the wall, in all the walls of my life, especially in my favourite long but narrow toilet; and I know you very well, you are terrible with me, me poor thing. Anyway, listen...

In the third island some interesting things are happening. Professor Cavallo and Palandro are animatedly debating a delicate matter. Their massive body-island floats beyond the piano, their world-sail full of wind. The professor's voice comes loudly from there: 'He was absolutely mad! He affirmed – I don't remember his precise words – that they did the deed, but it was we who had hoped it would be done. This is a disgusting thing.'

'Dear Professor, Baudrillard wasn't mad at all. He is a profound philosopher. In this case he explained his point of view very well. I don't remember the exact words either, they were more or less: I don't praise the murderous attacks – it would be foolish. I don't glorify them. I am trying to analyse the process by which globalisation produces its own death.'

'Are we speaking about the same author? The one that wrote about the end of history, about reality vanishing? These are silly things. The truth, the terrible truth, is that the Twin Towers collapsed with thousands of poor innocent people inside.'

Suddenly Cora emerges from her island, above the faded sea of bodies, a touch of the bird about her funny body, rich in strong colours, and trilling: 'Please, don't quarrel. This is a party. We must all be happy. And we ought to celebrate our leaving tomorrow. Please, keep quiet now, gentlemen.'

Suddenly, the bumptious schoolmistress flies over the same sea. She is a fat and horrible bird; with her slave, featherless and funny. She warbles in a contralto voice: 'Michele, my dear, you must write a poem on our departure. It should neither be too long nor too short. Now I'll think of the appropriate prosody for you; then, I will put your lines in a book of linguistic analyses and reflections about them, and about your being a poet. Are you happy?'

The featherless one sighs silently, and mumbles: 'I am not able to do it, Madam. Leave me alone, please. Leave me alone, please, please, please...'

Moving like a hen incapable of flying, like all hens, the waitress cries out her plan: 'I will make a huge oil painting for this departure, after Picasso's style.'

'It's impossible, dear. You don't know Picasso that well,' Cora says.

The people are speaking about so many things that the noise overwhelms me. I can't remember why we ought to go away or where we are going. Professor Cavallo looks at me, smiling, like a mischievous old boy.

4

FITZGERALDESQUE PARTY

Then there was a boom as Tom Buchanan shut the rear windows and the caught wind died out about the room, and the curtains and the rugs and the two young women ballooned slowly to the floor.

F. Scott Fitzgerald,
The Great Gatsby

And the two young women ballooned slowly towards the floor, and all things also ballooned to the floor now.

Well, who are those two women? One of them could be the young Evelina: yes, it's her. And close to me are the slave-poet and many elegant people. He is looking at me intensely. He has changed. He isn't calm, submissive and mute anymore. His appearance is detestable. I feel I hate him. And I try to go up to him to ask him where we are and why we are here; I think he knows many things. But he has disappeared through the crowd in the party.

Apropos of this party: a spider web of lights is above and underneath us so that this night is like dark blue silk dotted with sequins. Like the silk on the pliant bodies of those young women. The garden is big and surrounds an impressive neoclassical style villa. A monumental marble staircase goes down into the garden glittering in the multi-coloured lights, but conserving the dark mystery of its top. These are the twenties. My creation seems to prefer the jazz age. But let's continue describing the party. There are many tables under thick trees, where gentlemen and ladies are chatting, and where waitresses and waiters come and go around and inside the night, with their trays full of cups of Pineapple Champagne Punch. Good music comes from somewhere to the right side of the villa: Jelly Roll Morton and his Red Hot Peppers. They are on a marble platform covered in part by some trees with people dancing around them. There is a big swimming pool. And looking towards it I see a long snake of white lights all the way to a huge garden gate. At its head are four sleek cars. Now I'm here, by the gate, so I can see them properly: a 1929 light and dark red Desoto Roaster; a superb 1929 two-toned grey Pierce Arrow

Convertible Coupe; a 1929 white Chrysler Roaster and a 1929 water-green Ford Model A Phaeton.

I think, good work, indeed. If it's all mine. 1929. It must be summer, or late spring, and not only because it's warm. (Do you remember what happened in that October?) So this is the age I am living in now. Maybe. All these colours and yellow music and beautiful ladies have distracted my attention from the only important thing: that this is a cage, a marvellous jail, but a jail someone has put me in. My Enemy?

'I think I know you,' a pleasant woman says to me. It is the young Evelina.

'You might. You are Evelina, aren't you?'

'Yes. Where did I meet you?'

'It's difficult to answer. However I remember seeing you in a station with three men: a young man with pearl grey Oxford bags and a dark double-breasted jacket, and two other men. I have followed one of them so far,' I say prudently.

'Oh, it isn't important, dear. A friend of mine would like to meet you. Come to our table. She is a very charming person.'

Her face is lovely: oval, luminous, with slightly astonished eyes, a small mouth and a pretty, crooked nose. A beautiful woman. She looks elegant in her sand-coloured Coco Chanel and bob-cut. She is familiar to me, and this would be normal for me, but…

'Dear, here is an old friend of mine, my creator,' says Evelina from under her white cloche hat.

'How strange. Another writer.'

'I'm glad to meet you, madam. My name is Lorenzo, and, yes, I am a sort of writer.'

The beauty looks at me archly.

'I am Zelda. And it is a pleasure to meet you.'

I stop thinking about what Evelina has just said. I am interested in this Zelda now. It could be *that* Zelda.

'Are you a writer too?'

'Not really, dear. My husband is a writer, a good one they say, a genius. I am only a woman: I am a stupid creature, but I am a buttercup, aren't I?'

'Oh yes! Scott is great. Have you read his new novel?' Evelina thrills with delight.

'So Evelina, that means I am only a buttercup...'

'Don't be silly, Zelda. You are a very special person.'

A pause to reflect. My knowledge of the life of the most important American writers could be creating all this around me now. It could. But I didn't choose to be here. And that Michele, the slave-poet... Who is he? Who is he working for?

'Can I lead this gentleman out of this mess?'

With these words, a young man, handsome and elegant, interrupts the conversation.

'Egisto, you know Lorenzo?' asks Evelina.

'Like a father knows his son or vice versa.'

'Excuse me, ladies. I have to follow this gentleman.'

They have just finished playing *Black Bottom Stomp* and are starting with *Jungle Blues*. And in a true jungle of bodies we search for a track to the table full of cups of Pineapple Champagne Punch. (It's clear: my fantasy knows only this drink.)

'So you know me,' I say.

'Yes, very well too. You are a lucky man. You need my help now.'

It's pointless to try to find a solution with these clots of my blood in this crazy world of mine. My quiet thoughts follow incomprehensible laws. Yes, it's fantastic. I am enjoying myself.

'My dear Professor, I know your old version. It's different. But this may be a marginal consideration.'

'What drink would you like, old sport?' the young Egisto asks.

'I don't feel like one now, thank you.'

'Well. Yes, it is marginal. We must immediately solve another problem. We must return to our time to provide for the journey,' he says, and his voice seems older than his appearance; it is almost the voice of the old Egisto.

'But why is this journey so important?'

Two men dressed in black and holding huge chrome guns begin to shoot the guests. People shouting, run here and there, and someone is falling, wounded, close to us. It is a woman in yellow: a large gash is filled of red.

'Follow me, Lorenzo, be quick,' screams Egisto pulling me by the jacket.

'What's happening?' I scream in my turn.

You, my audience in the wall, you can bear witness that I hate violence and all types of weapons, and that blood fills me with repugnance. You know me very well. So we have the evidence that someone has invaded my world with work of his own. I can't be the author of that cruel scene. Now, as you can see, the young Egisto and I are running like the wind among tables and terrified people, and we end up in a dark, silent, hollow place. Above us (we are lying down) there are two tables, or perhaps only a large one. The floor is sticky and subsiding a little; there are neither stars nor lights nor sounds nor voices nor shots here...

'Welcome to this dark and silent spot, where the wise men are thinking about important things,' says a voice beside us.

'Oh, it's you Scott,' exclaims Egisto.

'At your service, Sir,' Scott says, and his voice seems to bend in fun.

'What are you doing here, old sport?'

'The same thing you and your friend are doing. But your friend might not know me. I think I should introduce myself. My name is Francis Scott Fitzgerald, but only Scott for you, if you want. I am a writer,' he says with mocking solemnity.

'It is an honour to meet you, Mr Fitzgerald... Scott. I am Lorenzo.'

Someone is snoring at the bottom of the hollow, a big shape near the writer.

'Is there a gentleman with us?' Egisto asks.

'Not quite, boy. It is Mr Capone,' answers Scott.

'Al Capone, the gangster?' asks Egisto.

'It is him. He was here before my arrival. I think he mistrusted his boys: bullets don't recognize him as a boss.'

'Apropos of this: Gatsby, our host, told me that a gangster he knows had something for my friend here,' says Egisto.

'Don't worry. He told me all about it. And that gangster is this one here.'

Once again, I don't understand at all. I would like to ask something about the shooting, but I prefer to wait, for now. They may speak about it.

'And Michele... did they manage to pinch him?' asks Egisto.

'No. He beat it out. He's terribly sly, you know what he's like,' Scott says.

So Mr Capone is at enmity with the slave-poet: so he is my friend, indirectly. What nice friends I have.

'Can I ask a question, gentlemen?' I say.

A pause. Then it is Scott who answers me: 'You should know everything about this, my friend. We were only joking for the sake of the audience in the wall, not for you, the creator; or rather their creator, seeing that I existed already as a notion in your mind from your youthful reading.'

'I don't know if I am the creator or a creature only.'

'Sometimes I don't know whether Zelda and I are real or whether we are characters in one of my novels.'

The door to return has opened. I think the party is continuing outside, as this adventure continues inside me.

5

FELLINESQUE PARTY

I think that bees were divine beasts too, because they vomit honey, even if someone says they take it from Jupiter. Therefore they prick: wherever sweetness is, you can find bitterness.

Gaius Petronius Arbiter,
The Satyricon

Dear audience in the wall, if I were a good creator I wouldn't repeat myself continuously, but I am not such a creator. I apologize for this. I will try to control myself and my creatures; adjust our behaviour. Professor Egisto Cavallo will help me to reach my goal. Well. It is a tepid (summer?) evening, and Evelina is playing a piece of music I know very well on the piano but I can't recall the title at present. It is pleasant music, maybe from a famous film. Coralba is in the garden under bright stars like cold eyes. The murmur of a nearby sea reaches us.

'We could speak about that thing on the deceptive swallows you saw this morning from your bed,' says Professor Cavallo. 'It is an interesting subject if you link it with the theories of a famous French sociologist and philosopher.'

'Whose?' I ask.

'Jean Baudrillard's.'

'Didn't you speak with Palandro about him?'

'Exactly. He likes Baudrillard immensely; as you do, don't you?' the professor asks.

Evelina goes on playing the same music. Yes, it is fine, but…

'I didn't even know his name before your discussion. What does he say about the deceptive swallows?' I ask.

'Nothing about the swallows, but much about deceptiveness. He argues for the death of reality killed by virtualization. For him – not for me – humanity ought to prepare to live in a virtual reality.'

That music is hurting my ears. It is agreeable music, but…

'Professor, but it's true, isn't it?' I say loudly over that music. 'These are fascinating thoughts. I would like to know more. Could you suggest some books?'

'*The System of Objects*, *The Consumer Society*, *The Mirror of Production*, *Forget Foucault*, these were written in his first period dedicated to 'object over the subject'; then, his fundamental book: *Simulacra and Simulation*, about 'hyper-reality', that is the simulated realm is 'more real than real…' Please, dear Evelina… can't you stop this music, *please*?'

Suddenly we are standing, moving like mechanical puppets to the window overlooking the meadow.

Professor Cavallo says: 'Don't worry, my friend. We will have sufficient time to speak about that… another time I think.'

Yes. A mechanical will is pushing us like a strong wind from hell. Yes. And the music? Now I remember what it is: that circus-style march from Fellini's *8½*. It is pushing us almost through the window, where the stars are shining and silence is singing.

'Friends, don't be upset, it's only a jest, a fanciful story,' Cora shouts from the meadow.

A *jeune faune* is following her, playing his Pan-pipes. Cora is not that young and naked she looks terrible, poor thing. Look, she is dancing like a bear. Oh my God! Next to me the professor is laughing, behind me Evelina is playing. To the notes of Nino Rota they are dancing round and round with people who are emerging from the dark. There, the serious Palandro, so elegant, so charming; Palandro arm in arm with The Girl Who Wants To Paint A Masterpiece; there, the fat Schoolmistress with her slave poet in a dark blue suit (so defenceless); there… the same people, partial people, incomplete, no arms, no legs, no heads, remember? And other people I don't know: peasants I think. These men and women are numerous, and the music is outside, it is there, played by a band, not

48

Evelina's piano. Evelina has gone out now and is dancing with them. It's a genuine village party.

'Come here, my friends,' calls Cora from behind her faun.

No. No. And no! For once I ought to impose my will. The window shuts by itself. Outside people continue their amusement without us. I turn towards Professor Cavallo. 'A little silence to speak for a moment.'

'Congratulations, Lorenzo, what you have done is remarkable. It isn't too late for you to become a serious god,' the professor says, smiling at me.

'You make a fool of me. But I grant that you're right about my power. It is feeble. I want to speak about that, connecting it with what you said before about that Frenchman and his theories, which resonate with my impressions.'

We have returned to the table and are sitting opposite each other.

'I don't understand what relations there are between your insufficient power and Baudrillard,' doubts the professor.

'There are, I'm sure. But you were saying something about his fundamental book…'

'Yes, *Simulacra and Simulation*. He explains what 'hyper-reality' is. The simulated realm 'more real than real'.'

'More real than real… In the realm of the real, what is the principal element?' I ask the old man, who is absorbed in his thoughts.

'I don't know, my *too* young friend. There are many important elements in that realm. What you are thinking is probably fundamental only for you. Your thoughts are not mathematic laws,' the professor explains severely.

'Not only for me, Professor. I may seem pompous, but this is indeed an important thing.'

'Well then,' he explodes, 'what is this incredible thing?'

'Antagonism, if you prefer a simple and moderate word; but rivalry, contrast, hate, and what derives from them, murder, war, battle, fighting are also good words to describe this thing, dear Professor.'

The professor laughs till he shakes. Then he says: 'I did say it was an interesting subject if you connected it with the theories of that famous Frenchman, but I was only referring to your sensations, and only in a very superficial way. I merely gave you a hint in speaking about those theories, but your power is completely unequal to Baudrillard's theories. You are making a mess, my dear young friend.'

I'm impressed. My shallow culture has produced this walking encyclopaedia. Okay, I give up.

'Let's forget it. But I want to speak about my power, without other matters.'

'All right, if you must,' he answers with resignation.

'Do you know who my Enemy is?'

'"Wherever sweetness is, you can find bitterness" – somewhere Petronio Arbitro wrote...'

I'm sorry, but this dialogue will have to wait. At the moment, three or four cannon shots drown out any conversation. The music has stopped, people are still. The party is over. At the window two astonished faces (ours) enquire of the people gathered there to have fun what is happening. But silence answers from the silence.

Three strange types have arrived. They are like pilot fish, in the sense that wherever they appear, sharks must also be somewhere close; in this case, evidently sharks that know how to shoot cannons. The strangers look like cylindrical batteries with very thin heads, arms and legs. I recognize them as my childhood cylindrical batteries. I used to play with them everyday. What were their names? Oh yes! Shoe, Suit and Sweat.

'Hey, you there!' I shout to the professor's surprise.

Several people turn towards me, but not those strange chaps, because they are busy explaining to others what happened before they arrived.

'Hey, Shoe, Suit and Sweat!' I shout again.

As a single man they move towards my window and as a single entity they demand to know what I want and how I know their names.

'You can't remember, but you were my toys when I was a child,' I explain quietly.

'That is very interesting, Sir, but we have big problems to solve at the moment,' they reply together. 'An enormous army left its ships on the shore and is advancing and converging to this village. You ought to escape now if you want to survive.'

Meanwhile the cannon continues its discourse, *boom, boom, boom*, its incomprehensible speech, *boom, boom, boom*: and I think I am going mad or, perhaps, becoming a gullible fellow who doesn't know what he wants and what he does. Who is my Enemy? I asked the professor earlier. It is all a dream or nightmare; yes, I know this, but I see wounded people coming from the thick dark of the night… dead people! Death from my mind, if it is only my mind doing all this.

Here we are again. I am repeating the same things again and again. I have become boring like this …*boom, boom, boom*…

'Everything is ready for our departure,' shouts Cora, appearing at the door.

…*boom, boom, boom*…

51

'The old Beardmore will be our ship and airship and submarine and...' the professor says proudly, talking about something I don't understand.

...*boom, boom, boom*...

'I don't understand at all (again), but the Devil has too many munitions to chat about anything just now,' I say.

A huge wooden trapdoor opens in the middle of the floor; we are climbing down a steep rickety wooden ladder. It's a dark hole. Down there a little flame (a candle, I think) glints and throws a feeble light on many dark figures surrounding a big car. It appears to be a satanic meeting. Not a word from the members of this strange club.

...*boom, boom, boom*... (but faraway now)

Evelina is lighting an oil lamp. I know those people around that black car very well: Palandro, The Girl Who Wants To Paint A Masterpiece (from now on, simply The Girl), the big Schoolmistress, Michele (is he a slave-poet only?), Coralba, Professor Cavallo and Evelina; finally Shoe, Suit and Sweat, those batteries.

...*boom, boom, boom*, and people screaming outside... (faraway, because of the thick walls of this cellar, which is maybe an old cattle shed)

I am thinking I ought to say something, but I feel like an actor who has forgotten his line. I don't even have the catchword. But those creatures of mine are waiting for some word from me, I know – from their creator. What a disappointing god I am.

'All of you are perhaps expecting me to save you from this cruel army, but I know nothing about it. It may not be cruel. You might not have to escape from it. In any case, you can't die. You are only in my mind. So you ought to help me, my friends, because I don't know what is right and what is wrong, here and now. Clots of my blood, that you are.'

'"I want a genuinely false reality, in which I can feel real". This is a sentence of yours, lad,' the professor says. 'Then you began seeing people (your faerie people) wounded and dead with your own eyes. Do you remember? You can also die, now and here. You are like us, here. So, as Leonardo da Vinci said. "Chi teme i pericoli, non perisce per quegli". / "Who fears perils doesn't perish for those."'

'Dear Professor, that's a fine sentence,' thrills Cora with a pirouette worthy of a ballet dancer.

As if Cora has started a reaction, all the bystanders shout their personal opinions of what I said and what the professor said, commenting on his remarkable culture. Some blame and some praise. For example, Palandro says: 'I don't know if that sentence is Leonardo's or not, but it is too obvious for a great man like him. You needn't have disturbed him to say a truism like this.'

Schoolmistress and her slave-poet step forward, and she says: 'My friend and I think the professor is right and Palandro is wrong. We think – isn't it true, dear Michele? – that Leonardo's sentence is fundamental to elucidating our situation in the right aspect. The great experience of that wise man shows us how the simple ideas of simple people contain great truths…'

Even Shoe, Suit and Sweat have something to say, and an enormous swarm of words is raised in that small circle of light and in the dense blackness; a buzzing in which it is possible to hear some single word or phrase. But…

…*BOOM, BOOM, BOOM…* (yes, they are close again now)

'I think, friends, we should leave immediately,' says Evelina calmly, in a break of silence.

A man I don't know emerges from the car. He is tall and thin as a straw. He has black hair, black eyes, an enigmatic expression on a long face, and is wearing a brown crumpled suit.

'Oh dear Mayer, is our old Beardmore ready?' the professor asks.

'Yes, my 1958 Beardmore Taxi is always ready,' the man answers.

'May I introduce a friend of mine and of us all?' says the professor.

That bare bone man turns to me with his immutable grey face.

'His name is Lorenzo,' continues the professor, 'and he is our creator.'

Mayer looks at me with the same wooden expression.

'I'm glad to meet you,' I say, holding out my hand.

'So, you are our creator. Well. But you can't have made my taxi. *He* is working well,' concludes Mayer getting into the car.

The example of the taxi driver propels the other people to move inside that black rattletrap. It is even without wheels. And we are too many. And I think it isn't a simple car: maybe a strange airplane, or ship, airship, submarine, as the professor told me before. And they are piling on-board hastily for the gunfire is getting nearer and nearer. One by one, all on the left side, The Girl, Schoolmistress, Michele, Palandro, Evelina, Coralba, Shoe, Suit and Sweat, and some nameless-people (or partial ones), magically disappear. There is only Mayer, at the driver's seat within.

'You go first, my dear Lorenzo,' the professor invites me. 'Get in from the left door, please. The right one is broken.'

So I get into the taxi as well.

The light brown leather back seat is stained with dark brown and black patches of grease and dust; and many slits make it expressive, as if it were cheerful because of all those grins. I can see these details by a high artificial light shining inside the car. There is a metal trapdoor between the back seat and the partition, against which the metal top of the taxi leans; it is all very clear. I'm going down a long metal ladder; the professor is following me carefully; it is full of quiet morning light here. I reach a floor...but it is the floor of a house... that I know very well: a stretch of path is framed by the window in front of a normal door; the other window overlooks the scant piece of meadow with three bent trees; there is also the upright piano without one lateral side.

'But this is Cora's house,' I exclaim.

'Yes, dear, would you like a cup of tea?' asks Coralba from the corner where they do the cooking.

Evelina is sitting at the piano and has a marvellous smile for me.

The professor has been looking thoughtfully at me; and now he says: 'Don't worry, Lorenzo. Everything is well. It is clear that you aren't used to these variations and continuous surprises yet. It's only a matter of time. I tell you again: don't worry! We will help you.'

'All right, you are very kind, but I ought to understand what is happening here, or else I will go crazy. For example, first we went down to reach the cellar and the taxi, then we went down again and we have come back up here… Please, explain to me how this can work,' I say with hopelessness in my voice.

'Our old Beardmore,' spells out the professor, 'is both the crows-nest and the pilot bridge of an enormous ship that includes our normal world fixed or stopped at ten in the morning (this includes – I know it's strange – the taxi itself): if you want, you can return to your home in your car straight away…if you don't like all of this. Or you can stop thinking, obviously…'

'No! I can't kill my creation.'

'Well. Another good way to explain this strange situation is that of the iceberg: it has, you know, a small peak that rises out of the water, but underneath it is huge. We journey visibly on our peak, the taxi. The old Beardmore reaches all the places where we must play…'

'*Play* in what sense?'

'In the sense of act.'

'So we will be a sort of theatrical company,' I say.

'Not *a sort*, but a true theatrical company. Our repertory is rich in great *pièces* from the greatest playwrights in the history of the theatre, Shakespeare, Molière, Goldoni, Ionesco, Eduardo De Filippo, Pirandello, Betti, Beckett …'

The Girl comes in shouting something.

'Listen to me, listen to me, please, listen how well I worked on my role.' So she starts:

"Sometimes she can close them no more: when she no longer feels the need of hiding her shame to herself, but dry-eyed and dispassionately, sees only that of the man who has blinded himself without…"

'Stop, stop, stop!' shouts the professor, 'It's terrible, my dear girl, terrible. You have a brilliant career as a female announcer, but this is drama. Do you know what it means?'

(Cora to me, whispering) 'Pirandello, you know? *Six Characters in Search of an Author.* A line spoken by the step-daughter. But she is terrible, poor thing. She is better as a painter, as you know.'

Now The Girl is crying like a baby.

'Professor Cavallo, believe me, please. I rehearsed and rehearsed... Believe me, please, Sir,' says The Girl.

Schoolmistress comes in. She looks around with a stern expression, then points to The Girl exclaiming: 'She is unfit to play, and it's obvious that I am the right actress for this role. I would like to persuade you, Professor, that it is so. You are our actor-manager...'

Apparently calm, the professor moves to the centre of the room, next to Schoolmistress, so big and tall and aggressive.

'I have always thought that you are a cultured and wise woman but, in this case, you are similar to a fat stupid innkeeper's wife.'

(Cora to me, whispering) 'She is a fat stupid innkeeper's wife. So self-important! It was high time someone brought her down a peg or two. What do you think, Lorenzo?'

The fat woman, her face purple, steps back speechless.

'Now, dear girl, stop crying. Try the other part of the line, please,' the professor invites.

She makes herself tidy, then tries it:

"Oh, all these intellectual complications make me sick, disgust me – all this philosophy that uncovers the beast in man, and then seeks to save him, excuse him... I can't stand it, Sir. When a man..."

But this line is bound to be interrupted. From the taxi (or the backstage?), Mayer's bass drowns out the bird voice of the girl announcing:

'First stop Lyons, in the year of grace 1655.'

6

A GOOD BEER WITH MOLIÈRE

Sinning in silence is not sinning.

Molière,
Tartuffe

The Manager – Slave-poet *(half angry, half amazed):* An author? What author?

The Father – Palandro: Any author, Sir.

The Manager: But there's no author here. We are not rehearsing a new play.

The Step-Daughter – The Girl *(vivaciously climbing the ladder):* So much the better, so much the better, Sir! We can be your new play.

One of the actors – A partial person *(among lively comments and laughter):* Oh, do you hear that?

We are peeping at the audience from backstage; numerous, with wonderful clothes. We can see some elegant and good-looking women in the front row. One of them is wearing a blue bodice and petticoat with white ribbons and a lace-trimmed kerchief pinned at her neck. Another, a gold-coloured bodice and petticoat. A blonde wears a flame-coloured satin gown without a collar or kerchief, but a fur piece draping over her shoulder.

'Oh, what beautiful garments. This is a splendid century,' says Cora behind us.

'Ssh,' says the professor. 'They are working. You can look for a dressmaker – or better a *seamstress* – when the performance finishes if you want.'

'Our theatre is full of people tonight. Shoe, Suit and Sweat did a good job with those trumpets and drums around the streets of Lyons. And your idea, Professor. Great! It is simply a wonderful idea to stage a comedy by Pirandello in the seventeenth century,' I say.

'It's a pity we haven't the right clothes for this age. Shoe, Suit and Sweat went out in the wrong suits.'

'Yes, but they would have been three strange chaps in any case, dear Professor,' I say.

The theatre is in the inside-park – which, as you know, is both within and under the taxi, which in turn is in the cellar, that in turn... It is a small, disused porno cinema, still displaying its prurient bills from the last film, and close to Carlone's villa. The black locomotive, not to mention all the other things, captures people's attention, once they come through the Beardmore box-office where Mayer makes an efficient attendant. There is another touring company in Lyons at this time: Molière's. They are staging a new and cheerful comedy called *L'Etourdi*. But the Lyonese apparently prefer our *Six Characters in Search of an Author*.

The Father (hurt and mellifluous): Oh sir, you know well that life is full of infinite absurdities, which do not even need to appear plausible, since they are true.
The Manager: What the devil is he talking about?
The Father: I appreciate it may well be considered madness, yes Sir, to strive to do the contrary. I mean to create plausible situations so that they appear true. But permit me to observe that if this be madness, it is the sole *raison d'être* of your profession, gentlemen.
(The actors look restless and indignant.)

'He is in the stalls,' the professor whispers.
'Who?'
'Molière!'
I asked about him because I hadn't seen him in the third row. But I know Molière. Yes, I know him. A flashback is needed. This afternoon I was following those three chaps, Shoe, Suit and Sweat, when I met Molière. I wanted to watch them with their drums and trumpets in the old streets of Lyons to amuse myself a little. We (they in front of me and unaware of my presence) were walking along the right bank of the

Saône in the Saint-Jean quarter. It is a beautiful place full of Renaissance palaces, carriages, horses, ladies and gentlemen; and poor grey faced people that shuffled along in the elegant crowd. There was a gilded and no doubt comfortable coach in front of me; its body suspended by leather straps extended from a fixed assembly to the wheel axle. The coachman sat over the smaller front-wheels; some gentlefolk were looking out through the windows from within the body. That coach was so agreeable that it engaged my attention completely and I lost contact with the batteries walking among the people.

To be honest, I am often distracted in my life. And this state – that I could define as the normal disposition of my mind – always meets with some source of distraction. In this case, it was two wonderful buildings. The gothic Saint-Jean Cathedral and the basilica of Notre-Dame de Fourvière. As usual my fantasy fails when it entertains intricate details, though these are major details. (Though there is always the notion that the Enemy entered my world and got the details wrong – always a valid suspicion.) But, the basilica is a big mistake, because they will not erect it until 1872. My guidebook says this clearly. (I didn't know I had a guidebook in my pocket.) Well, it makes no difference to me, and, still, this was good work in general, I thought. But I had lost my friends, because of the roving speculations that crowded my mind.

At this point, cries came to help me from nearby. I turned to the left into a *traboule*, a passage used by the weavers to transport their silk goods from one street to the other. I ran toward those cries and saw others running like me. The passage ended in a large crowded street. An old woman was screaming, surrounded by worried-looking gentlemen. She was lying on three of them, as though on a comfortable human mattress. Shoe, Suit and Sweat stood there, in front of her. They were dumbfounded, holding their trumpet, drum and parchment scroll from which they had recently proclaimed: "Hear! Oh hear! Dear citizens of Lyons, hear! oh hear! Our dear audience, hear! This evening The Cavallo Touring Company is staging a new comedy by Luigi Pirandello, a great Italian playwright. Come to see *Six Characters in Search of an Author* by Luigi Pirandello at six o'clock. Come to see this masterpiece in Place des Terreaux ..." Etcetera.

That old lady must have observed them more closely than others had. They are, as you know, rather strange. The suits they wore were beside the point.

That poor woman, as I was saying, was screaming. Then other men and women noticed my odd friends and were amazed. Three or four ladies started screaming like a chorus supporting the first old lady, the soloist. Some of the men looked set to get angry at the sources of such insufferable strangeness. Two knights drew swords. The situation was escalating, but not for my friends, because I have never seen a battery that could die. In fact I'd never come across any other batteries that could live either, so my knowledge of them is limited, but I could not imagine a battery bleeding due to an inch of cold steel.

No, I was concerned only about myself. From time immemorial, and everywhere, when people get angry they blame foreigners; besides, I had on the wrong suit for the period, as you know. So I hid hastily in an inn bustling with people and noise. Nonetheless a problem remained that needed to be solved immediately. I had neither *Louis d'or* nor *Louis d'argent*.

There was half-light within. I sat at a long wooden table on a bench, hoping that nobody would come to ask me what I wanted to drink. There were many people, as I said, and I remained calm and quiet.

'You seem to be in difficulty, Sir. Can I help you?'

He looked exactly as he does in that famous painting by Pierre Mignard.

'You are very kind. I do have a little problem. I've forgotten my money bag.'

'Don't worry about it. I would like to buy a foreigner a pint of good beer. For a playwright is always interested in sticking his nose into odd situations,' Molière told me.

'It is an honour to meet a great playwright like you, and to give him an opportunity to exercise his rare gift. But I am not so odd as you think. I am a common person with a common life.'

Molière smiled at me. 'My dear sir, it's strange that you know me... Anyway, I'm not so important as you think. Besides, I am an actor more than a real playwright. Yes, I wrote some comedies, but...'

'You will become a great man, and not only in your own country,' I declared.

'Are you a wizard?' Molière said, laughing. 'Anyway, you are kind to me. Thank you very much. Well, would you like something to drink now?'

'With great pleasure.'

A man brought us two beers. Outside people were quiet now. Maybe Shoe, Suit and Sweat could escape. They didn't have so many problems after all. Molière observed me intensely so that I felt a little embarrassed.

'Excuse my curiosity, but your garments are strange. I suppose those three odd chaps are your friends.'

'Which odd chaps are you speaking about?'

'Didn't you come in when that woman was screaming in the street? So, you must know what I mean.'

'Ah, those. Yes, they are strange. I agree with you, *Monsieur* Molière'

'I'm glad your memory is good, dear friend.'

'No one ever compared me to a battery,' I exclaimed, laughing.

'A battery? What is that?'

Evidently not all my characters know more than me about my world. Or, maybe, Molière was lying for some reason I don't understand.

'Sinning in silence is not sinning,' said Molière as though acting on stage.

'I beg your pardon?'

He looked at me with a quizzical expression.

'Strange! I didn't intend to say that sentence. I don't know what it means. Maybe you know something about it?'

'Yes, I suppose I do. Do you know *Monsieur* Tartuffe?'

'Yes. But what does it mean? I don't understand.'

How could he know Tartuffe, a character from a play that he will not write for many years? It was strange, indeed.

'So you are the man whom Tartuffe was speaking about,' said Molière.

Surely you all know the treasure hunt, the game where people search for something hidden. They have numbers on their backs, or on their cars. It seems my imagination decided to create this story woven together with that stupid game. Like a harlequin dress. I hope you comprehend. Apparently I am not the prime mover of all this, as you know. So now we fiddle while Rome burns. Let us return to the theatre, and to the inn, immediately.

'Now I understand everything,' I exclaim.

'So, we should beware of the false friend. Molière? Tartuffe?' Professor Cavallo says. 'This is a difficult problem, my young friend.'

'The Bard and the Enemy. Good and evil. Too simple.'

'The true reality is not more intelligent than ours,' retorts the professor.

'I agree. But this cheap spy story is ridiculous. Can't we reach the house of the Bard with a good map?' I say.

'I don't know. I only know that he sent someone with a message for us about the directions we must use to reach the next stop here in France and through time,' the professor patiently explains.

That afternoon I didn't know all this, so I had been surprised to hear Molière speaking in that way.

I answered him: 'No, I don't know *that* Tartuffe! What are you talking about?'

Molière looked at my face. He didn't say anything else, only stared at me intensely, as if he hoped to read my soul. Then he changed subject.

'Do you belong to The Cavallo Touring Company?' he asked me.

'Yes, I do'

'Is Pirandello alive?'

Here was an easy question at last, paradoxically. It was easy to be quite honest... paradoxically again. Because he was not born yet, it was easier to say: 'No, he isn't.'

'What a pity.'

'Pirandello is essentially like you,' I said.

'That's interesting. But what does it mean?'

So let me explain what I said, or better, what I tried to say to my new friend: both Pirandello and Molière broke the conventions of their age. This is simple. It was difficult to explain to Molière the conventions Pirandello had broken, but the madness of my imaginary world came to my aid when he answered himself.

'He takes his fundamental ideas from Bergson. Reality is a perpetual vital movement. Whatever takes on a distinctive and individual form begins to die.'

Astonishing! Molière was explaining Pirandello to me.

'Every form is a mask that man imposes on himself and that society imposes on him. Pirandello walked down the path in the opposite direction to me. For me: from masks to men; for him, from men to masks.'

'So, you know Pirandello better than me,' I said.

'It's strange, I don't know what has happened. Maybe I knew what I said, yet I felt like an instrument in someone's hand.'

Don't worry, my dear audience in the wall. Maybe my fantasy wants to imitate reality. We all are like a shop with a marvellous window but without a decent storeroom. And culture, you know, is always within the storeroom. If I had had a bigger storeroom in my mind I would have thought of a better story than this one. More linear, I think. The tragedy is that my window isn't that good. Poor me. But the inn is more important than these superfluous thoughts of mine. Our inn full of smoke and noise, and our fine Molière with his big storeroom stuffed with culture... who was saying with fervour: 'I like realistic situations and I try to get deeply inside my characters, I want to pass criticism of so-called noble folk's behaviour. They are ridiculous sometimes, aren't they? I have some excellent ideas on the subject.'

'Be careful, *Monsieur*, the road you chose is a dangerous one. There could be a jail at the end of it. Aristocrats don't like criticism,' I said.

Some Actors: He's dead! Dead! Poor boy!
Other Actors: No, no, it's only make believe, it's only pretence!
The Father (standing and shouting): Pretence? Reality, Sir, reality! *(He disappears behind the backdrop. Desperate.)*
The Manager (exhausted): Pretence? Reality? To hell with it all! Lights! Lights! Lights! (The stage is suddenly illuminated.) Never in my life has such a thing happened to me. I've lost a whole day over these people, a whole day!
CURTAIN

The audience burst into applause. It is a matryoshka of theatres, as you know. One within another, within another, etcetera. The actors bow, after the curtain has opened again. In the front row those elegant women are especially excited. In the third row, there is Molière; also clapping enthusiastically. Two rows behind him there is a man dressed in black, with a long grey face, too serious and still. His name is Tartuffe, as you can imagine; he is *deadly* serious. How do I know? I am the creator…sometimes.

'It is a great success, Professor,' I say. 'Incredible. People of this age like Pirandello, or better understand him. Incredible indeed.'

'Maybe it is, but enjoy it just the same; you are never satisfied, young man. Your deliberations about the strangeness that happened here are annoying at times – this is your world. Don't forget it. You are like the bore that criticises a film so much that he loses all taste for seeing the film itself.'

'Okay, I grant that you're right.'

As the colourful and strange audience finished clapping, a woman began to scream. Why was she screaming? You ought to know. I told you before when I was speaking of Tartuffe. Yes. He is the reason for her screaming, or rather his dead body. Tartuffe, with his black clothes and grey face, is dead, his face greyer than ever. Let's listen to her.

'He's dead! He's dead! My God, he is dead! My God! I faint! I faint....'

Etcetera. She is as big as a large wardrobe. Can you imagine her? And can you imagine what sort of mess there is now? A chorus of women, not all as big as this one, but all sufficiently noisy to make a memorable din. Incredibly, I am speechless. Therefore, I decide irrevocably:

Let the curtain go down on this comedy.

7

SWEET CHARLOTTE

'You who make the laws, the vices and the virtues of the people will be your work.'

Louis de Saint-Just, Autumn 1792

I am a faithful man. Especially to my wife. Because I have a wife in the... real world, out of this mad world of mine, made with pieces of me. It's important to make this point clear. I want to have a clear conscience. Like all honest men, I am vulnerable on this issue, anxious about threats from the wide crooked world. What happened yesterday, and this morning in part, is a serious mistake. I must unburden my mind of an oppressive thought. But first I ought to tell you calmly of my recent ups and downs.

I found myself alone in a Paris so different from the one I knew, and in the middle of a revolution: *pardonne moi*, The Revolution. The professor insisted on staging another of Pirandello's comedies, but this Pirandello was most inappropriate for the historical moment. It was about a crazy man that thought (or feigned) he was a famous king from the past. It is not at all pro-monarchy, but it's impossible to reason with fanatics and their guillotine in a climate of terrible excitement caused by daily bloodshed. The first evening Robespierre came with Palandro, his friend and fan. On the second evening he preferred to send the *Gendarmerie Nationale*. They arrested most of my friends. I don't know how many of them were arrested. I managed to escape in the night, such a strange night, so far away in space and in time.

And suddenly I felt that sensation – a cold wind blowing inside me – and it captured me and didn't leave me anymore until she smiled. But let's proceed in an organized manner. I slept in a cellar, and then at five in the morning I went out. People were waiting for the bakers' shops to open. A good smell of bread in the air made me happy, but the people stared at me. They stood there, queuing for bread, many of them facing me with expressions of disapproval on their faces. What were they thinking? Maybe they suspected that I was an enemy of the Revolution, one of those actors who loved cruel kings and dissolute queens. Strange! In this Paris events that took place in one quarter could go unknown in another. I discovered this in an interesting book by James Maxwell Anderson called *Daily Life During the French Revolution*. I read it some years ago (in the real world). I didn't know which part of the city I was in and I couldn't remember the place where we had played Pirandello. But I wandered far that night. This time I had the right suit on, the one I'd worn on the stage against the professor's wishes. He would have liked us to have neutral black and white stage costumes, but they were too modern for this corner of history. That's so like him! Even in a crazy place like this Egisto Cavallo distinguishes himself as an original.

Well, I was speaking about the hostility from the Parisians. I think their displeasure was a parody of my real life. You should know that I am terribly unpleasant. People normally hate me on first meeting, and sometimes at first glance. By the second glance they may try to kill me. I have a face that wears a mask of perpetual disgust. If I try to smile, a grimace blooms. So, these reactions are normal for me. But not here. Here, among my beloved almost-people. That must be why I immediately noticed her benevolent eyes among those face-aches. But I will tell you about her later, after a brief lesson on how you can find a good Parisian café during the Revolution.

My information on this matter is remarkable, thanks to that book, I think. So I knew where to find some excellent cafés in the city. I didn't know the city itself, but that was not a problem. I never need to know a place; some intuition always takes me where I would like to go. It was afternoon and I craved a cool drink. There were two criteria for the choice of a café: political leanings or characteristic specialities. You needed the first criterion for Café Corazza (the Jacobins' meeting-place), Café des Arts (the extremists' haunt), Café de la Victoire (the moderates' place), Régence (for Lafayette's friends) and Café de la Monnaie (for his enemies). But I am indifferent to party matters, and not only in this age. Then there was Café Caveau (a good place for an insurrection), Grottes Flamandes (excellent beer), Café Mécanique (with it's curious mechanical devices) and Café de Foy (rather trendy, I would say) were interesting for their distinctiveness. For me such diversions are better than political affiliations, and I could have chosen one of them, maybe the Grottes Flamandes because I like beer very much, but instead I went to the Café de la Porte St. Martin, where quiet people got together for a chat after an evening walk. I'm a quiet man too. I hate violence and, to be honest, revolutions when people shed blood like water.

As soon as I entered, a man, maybe the owner, came towards me with a big smile, opening his arms as if he wanted to welcome his best friend.

'*Merci, Monsieur* Lorenzo, *merci mon ami*! Your gift is wonderful. Our patrons are most enthusiastic. We knew the Café Mécanique had it for a long time, but...'

'Excuse me, *Monsieur*, but I don't understand. What are you speaking about? What is this precious gift I have given you?' I asked him.

It could have been the tone of my voice, more likely my unlovable face, or perhaps something else in my behaviour, but the owner gave a terrible look at me as if

75

I had given him an unwelcome gift. He turned his back on me and mingled with the patrons and patronesses, who shared his hostility for me. A forest of glares surrounded me; everyone was against me in that pleasant café.

She was sitting at a table by a window. She looked at me with an enigmatic (but kind) expression. As I told you before, I immediately noticed her because it was as if she had carved a niche with her cheerful colours amongst that grey-black hostility. Therefore, at the outset of my Mistake I was not so guilty. I couldn't have spoken with anybody else, as you can see. And then, she was the first to speak. (I am sorry to split hairs about all that has happened, but I am within my rights to do so in self-defence).

She started like this: '*Monsieur*, you ignore the latest rumours about our cafés. Please, sit down at my table, so I can tell you all about them.'

Here is the point I fear to reach. How can I describe the innumerable sensations I felt, visual, auditory, olfactory and (alas!) tactile? One step at a time, I think. I prefer to begin with what I would define as the cold parts of this matter; the neutral, innocuous parts. Clothes, for example. She seemed a gentlewoman, a young lady… a beautiful young lady. She was young, not like me. The professor keeps saying I am young, but I am not. At the age of fifty (my age) you are certainly young for old people and certainly old for young ones. So, covering all that bright youth of hers (she was twenty-five at the most) I noticed an ivory plain-sleeved chemise dress with a narrow brown sash. She had a mass of chestnut curls under her large straw hat, worn at a rakish angle. Her hair was already a danger zone for me. I can also tell you about hot and perilous parts of this lady. The eyes, so deep, dark and large, seemed to engulf me: a gentle and womanly pit. I don't know if it was a hell or a heaven; but I can tell you about this ambiguous feeling that came afterwards. The description is almost finished, as are these obvious metaphors caused by my deep disturbance. Listen! On that perfect oval face of hers, a small and regular nose was set nicely above thick lips that seemed to call for my masculine (and not so tired) essence.

'Yes, with great pleasure,' I answered, sitting down. 'You are very kind.'

'I am only a woman that wants to chat a little with a man that seems to be a nice person,' she said in her beautiful voice. 'Well, can you see this bent metal tube at the corner of the table?'

'Yes, I can'

'If you wish, you can have your mocha pumped directly into your cup thanks to this hollow leg. It's fantastic, isn't it?'

'Yes, it is nice. But the owner was talking about a gift I had given him… I don't understand.'

'Maybe you preferred this café to Café Mécanique.'

Her explanation called for some prudence on my side. It was clear: I had done something (was it that mocha tube?), or someone else had done it for me without my permission. My Enemy? Perhaps I gave Café de la Porte St. Martin that thing, thinking it was unfair that only Café Mécanique should have such a device.

'I think all Parisian cafés should have these marvels of technology.'

Had I just spoken of prudence? Well, I immediately did something rash.

She looked at me questioningly. Then she said: 'Café Mécanique has changed its name. It is now called Café Le Vol.'

'*Le vol?* Did someone steal something from there?'

'Yes, as you very well know. Didn't you steal this marvel of technology from Café Mécanique?' the young woman asked.

In some cases it is better to let the matter drop. So I did. Something helped me. There was a book on the corner of the table opposite the mocha corner. Here a good occasion to change subject.

'Were you reading that book before I arrived?'

'Yes. Do you know Plutarch? This is his best book: *Parallel Lives.*'

Oh my God, another cultured character in this odd adventure of mine. I never meet simple people who are more ignorant than me. Never! Always geniuses or learned men. Or beautiful women that read Plutarch. Well. Now I had to try to make a good impression. If I put this Plutarch in my work I had to know something about him. And sure enough – like a child with red cheeks and the enthusiasm to perform on his birthday, his head stuffed with the words of a poem he has learnt – I threw all this out:

"Now, Antony had a trusty slave named Eros. Him Antony had long before engaged, in case of need, to kill him, and now demanded the fulfilment of his promise. So Eros drew his sword and held it up as though he would smite his master, but then turned his face away and slew himself. And as he fell at his master's feet Antony said: 'Well done, Eros! Though thou was not able to do it thyself, thou teaches me what I must do.'"

'I see that you know it very well,' the girl said with an ironic smile.

No comment about this. You know everything. I can only say that her beauty appeared to be a physical thing that I could touch, if I wanted to. The look on her face alarmed me, suggesting some deep connection already existed between us.

'Would you like something to drink, Lorenzo?'

'Oh, you know my name.'

'The owner said it before, when you came in through the door.'

'Oh yes, yes, I didn't remember. And you, what is your name?'

'Charlotte. And the beer?'

'Oh yes, I like you...' I blurted like a stupid spotty-faced adolescent.

'I beg your pardon?'

'Beer, I like it very much. Beer, obviously, beer.'

'Obviously? That's not nice of you, Lorenzo.'

I wished I could stop the situation, the conversation in particular, but it was impossible. Now that everything has happened, I can do it. Or rather, I need to stop it for a while to allow for reflections about myself, and her. At that moment, in Café de la Porte St. Martin nothing particular was happening; only me as usual, the simple part of *me*: benches, tables, quiet people drinking and doing normal things, the light of the day outside before the evening, that particular orange air that wraps everything lightly like the veil of an evening gown. But the other part of me (her part) was a problem. It was too complicated. Nothing could justify what I felt: not her eyes, that hair, nor all her shining youth. She was me! The problem and solution were one. She was an imaginary person; insubstantial as air; a mere character of mine. But there was something wrong and it was disturbing. Caution. That was necessary, much prudence... with myself.

Well. What happened then? Oh yes. She tapped a cup of coffee through the hollow table leg while I had my cool and foamy good beer in a jug. I had forgotten

79

that something had come to my aid. The arrival of the beer, brought by the owner himself, and of the coffee, brought by the magic of modernity, imposed a break in that perilous conversation. I didn't want to answer that young woman... Charlotte. So I spoke about the book again.

'What do you think of *Parallel Lives*?'

'I don't know. I think it's interesting because it describes common and very human vices and virtues,' Charlotte answered, trying to remain serious; but a smile bent her mouth.

'"The vices and the virtues of the people will be your work,"' I reeled off.

'Where did you hear that sentence?' asked the young woman, suddenly serious.

'I must have read it somewhere. I don't remember,' I said, worried by her change of mood.

(Why was I anxious if she was nothing to me?)

'But do you know who said those words?'

'No. Is it that important?'

'The blood of innocents, I think, is very important.'

'Well, who is...?' I exclaimed.

'One that deserves the guillotine: Louis de Saint-Just.'

We noticed that the owner was standing by our table in silence.

'Would you like to ask anything, patron?' said Charlotte.

'*Mademoiselle*, you should be leaving.'

'*Merci*, that's very kind of you.'

The owner turned away like a rigid tin soldier, then returned to the spot without looking at me, still rigid like a tin soldier.

Along that street, men and women had been hung in the last light of the day. They had removed the oil lamps: the corpses couldn't have lit our walk, I think. This was evidently the reason for the owner's kind concern for Charlotte and something compelled me to be kind too.

'Can I accompany you to your hotel, Charlotte?' I asked, repenting immediately for having said this.

'At this point two roads could be chosen: NO, I don't want to risk it; YES, why not? You decided on the right road, in my opinion. I hoped you would offer to walk me to my hotel,' she said with a marvellous smile that summed up her glittering and disquieting youth.

She lodged at Hôtel de la Providence, located at no. 19, rue Vieux Augustin, not too far from Place des Victoires. Just twenty minutes on foot from this macabre street, but she preferred to catch a cab. Everything was too quick for me. Probably it was my inexperience that made this romantic affair so clumsy. And I didn't want to do anything with that girl. Really! You must believe me!

But when we arrived at the hotel, she asked me: 'Are you sure you want to come up?'

I don't remember what I answered, but we went up to the second floor, where she had a room.

I felt like an American actor in an old Hollywood movie – who would you prefer, Robert Mitchum, Kirk Douglas, James Stewart? – and, obviously,   after everything had happened... In those films you only imagine the spicy details. It was the same for me this morning. I was naked in a large bed under a heavy wood headboard, I could see her bare shoulder and a head full of brown curly hair peeping the blankets; she was lying face down. I ought to have imagined what I had done with her in the night, if I had done anything, because I didn't remember. Then I fell asleep.

I first woke early in the morning, remaining still, full of fear and regret in the dark. The noise of plodding hooves came from outside. The farmers pulled their carts towards the central market. I knew where I was. And with whom I was. I heard the young woman breathing. Sometimes she moved under the blankets, and I prayed she wouldn't touch me and wake up. She had to be quiet in her dreams and forget my existence. I felt physically ill. I was sweating, but, I rationalised, *it is July*. No, it was my terrible guilt.

By the time I opened my eyes for the third time, the room was full of daylight and noises from the street. I thought it was ten or eleven in the morning, maybe later. I didn't look at her. I didn't do anything. I remained supine, rigid, breathing sometimes, staring ahead of me. An opalescent bubble of silence took shape around me. I felt a great attraction to this simple, small, comfortable place: Jonah's whale, as Jung would say, is a metaphor for the womb, a safe place in which you can crouch far from the world, from history; a place where you can choose unity instead of multiplicity, the Mother instead of the Father. Because Charlotte represented the opposite of this in my odd world: she threatened to become a piece of reality, *too real*, with all of reality's menacing problems for a fragile, neurotic man like me. Charlotte was too strong; I had met something *too real* in my fantastic world and perhaps I would meet something else even stronger. In fact, I know I will. And even if Jung says to me: 'Be careful, lad, the whale is always hungry, your aspiration to drown in your own spring is so strong that it is a kind of suicide.' I can retort: "Listen to me, old wise man: here, in my odd home, I do what I want."

From my opalescent bubble, I could see, through a pleasant window I had made, a bureau on which there

82

was a branched candlestick without candles, and a book. What did the book mean, if it was *that* book? Was she still in the bed beside me? At that moment I realized I couldn't hear anything, neither her breathing, nor her movements under the blankets. With a great effort, I turned onto my left side, splitting the now useless bubble. The bed was strangely empty; that is, it was both empty and full of something. And I felt sad and relieved at the same time. She had gone; maybe she had left the book for me to have a keepsake of hers... because I took for granted it was that book ... No, all this is ridiculous. She was only a character, an imagination in my odd world. I must never forget this fundamental truth. She was a bit of air.

I didn't have *francs germinal*, only French coins of the twentieth century. Luckily, Charlotte had paid for the hotel. Before I left a strange thing happened to the book, which was *Parallel Lives* by Plutarch, as I thought. When I decided I should leave it in the room, the book thought to disappear. It (he? she?) left a white stain on the bureau. Was it a suicide? Maybe. Everything is possible here. If anything similar to a man does exist, then it is a book, full of words like the human mind, and sometimes with bad ideas, like suicide.

Anyway, I was alone in the Parisian crowd again. Suddenly I felt as if a big hand (or strength) had released me and I was free to think again. Charlotte had pushed me into a corner, and all my thoughts had been in her realm. Now my friends' problems re-emerged in my mind so that what began as a welcome feeling of liberation changed to sheer desperation. Robespierre – remember? – had sent the *Gendarmerie Nationale* to arrest my companions, and I didn't know how many of them had managed to escape. Nor could I do anything for those who were in the *Conciergerie*, from where few ever emerged alive. It's superfluous to tell you how I knew they were there. I know everything and I don't know anything, like anybody in the world, even mine. My world is a laboratory in which I can attempt innumerable human combinations using good and simple models – think of the water molecule: isn't it as clear as a toy?

Yet this is not a game for children. A person can die here. I thought this as I went to the Palais Royal gardens and saw her alone on a bench. She had a bundle by her, on the bench, and looked so serious, so intent on something, that her expression reminded me of when I had spoken that sentence about vices and virtues: an impenetrable look, filled with hostility towards the whole of humankind, a wall too high to climb, for me, for anyone, I think. Then I felt I hated her. And I didn't do anything to attract her attention. But Charlotte was looking at me; I was looking at her. Anyway, she was so beautiful. There is something strange in these moments... a lump in the throat. Moments in which a story finishes...

Well. My latest reflection was nonsense. Think nothing of it. Did I say that she was looking at me? It was clear she didn't recognise me, because her way of looking indicated: *why are you staring at me? I don't know you.*

Maybe that young woman wasn't Charlotte, after all.

8

A NARRATORS' MEETING

Woman is born free and lives equal to man in her rights.
Social distinctions can be based only on the common utility.

Olympe de Gouges,
The first article of the Declaration of the Rights
of Woman and the Female Citizen, 1791

I was tired. After I left Charlotte – if she was Charlotte – I walked along the streets and the squares of Paris. My fatigue came from desperation and tedium. Streets and squares were only the neutral streets and squares of a neutral city in a neutral time. As at the beginning of my mad journey, at times things and people disappeared into the deep and uniform white of my boredom. I thought I must stop all this mayhem and finally return to reality. Each step was too hard for me, like a difficult climb; an ascent in my empty, lazy, but anxious mind. Yet evening came as a motherly caress calming my fears; a new serenity that soothed my troubled mind, and something attracted me back to the Palais Royal gardens. I returned to the same point, to the same bench, but saw it with new eyes.

So here I am: I'm looking at the professor. There is no hurry to do anything to get him to notice me. Even I should be surprised by his presence in this place. But what I am interested in now is the ambiance. This quiet atmosphere that recalls my childhood when, on autumnal evenings, the electric yellow light collected itself within my room, imbued with rubber smells and the scents of other school things, pencils, workbooks, rulers... Your adventure world lives in your mind, sheltered against the large and hostile world of adults. Your mother looks at you with warm love... This, maybe because the professor is speaking about something, as a professor, lecturing invisible people ranged in front of him. I can't hear what he is saying, but I know it must be about French history. I risk getting nearer in order to hear him better. As I imagined, he is informing someone of the countless mistakes in my imagination – historical ones, obviously.

'...for example, I heard that tonight they will guillotine Louis de Saint-Just. This is wrong as well, because he was guillotined on 10 Thermidor An II (that is 28th July 1794), but today is 7 Thermidor An II (that is 25th July 1794). Then today Jean-Paul Marat was killed in his bathroom. This is also wrong. The assassination of Marat took place on 13th July 1793. The murderer was a young woman and this is correct, but it seems they will guillotine her with Saint-Just tonight. Another terrible error. There was a trial and her head was removed from her body four days after the murder...' the professor is explaining, while I have the strange sensation that I ought to know something about that young woman.

'You are right about my deplorable mistakes, Professor. And your explanation is clear and very interesting. But I don't see anybody listening to you now. Where is your audience?'

'Oh dear, dear Lorenzo! So, you managed to escape. Marvellous! I was so worried. I feel better now, much better indeed. Well, did you ask about my invisible audience? Yes, there is an audience, it is your dear audience in the wall, as always. There are school-age children in your audience, I think. You seem to forget that I am a retired teacher. Your world is a scandal, full of dreadful historical errors. It is a bad example for young people. I am trying to rectify some of your mistakes.'

'It's a good idea, Professor. But... listen... That young woman...'

'Yes?'

'Her name is Charlotte, isn't it?' I ask in a strained voice.

'Exactly, my lad. Marie-Anne Charlotte de Corday d'Armont (27th July 1768 to 17th July 1793), or, simply, if you prefer, Charlotte Corday. In 1847, the writer Alphonse de Lamartine will give her a famous nickname: Angel of Assassination... Do you feel unwell?'

Yes, and my face is white, terribly white. I'm turning pale, and you know why.

'Professor, did Charlotte have a book with her?'

'Yes, dear, a copy of Plutarch's *Parallel Lives*. What is wrong, Lorenzo?' says Egisto Cavallo; he looks worried.

'No, it's all right. I am only tired, very tired. Don't worry about me, Professor.'

Maybes crowd my thoughts now: *maybe* she was *Mademoiselle* Corday; *maybe* I made love to the Angel of Assassination. Somehow this eliminates another piece of reality from the love affair that was so improbable for me, for my faithful man's conscience. Every exaggeration obliterates itself. What was already merely a bit of air, is now lighter than ever in my mind. I feel relieved. And *maybe* nothing happened, all things considered. I am telling myself all this behind a smile; a mask that at first is false and then becomes truer and truer as my soul becomes lighter and purer, like air. I suspect myself of being a hypocrite. But *maybe* I am only a man.

That wise man knows me very well, so he is imagining I had been in some peculiar situation. He sees my reluctance to speak about it, so immediately changes the subject, telling me what happened to him in the last few days. His voice, you know, is always calm but, sometimes, too professorial. His way of narrating is ordered and worthy, and shows a particular attention for details; at the same time he knows the art of cutting out all the things that aren't important in an intelligent account. You will certainly prefer to listen to his voice:

A flight always leaves a mess around you. I don't know what happened precisely. And my adventure through the city was dull. Only the last episode is remarkable; I wish to give all my attention to this because an incredible thing took place. But I don't like to over-dramatise. So I will say, in plain words, that I met Michele, the slave poet, after a series of banal events. He was pretending (at least this is what I thought) to sell strange hats in a crowded market. I must be honest with you, Lorenzo. I showed an excessive interest in these hats becoming to the point of seeming ridiculous, but I recognised Michele and I hoped he wasn't an enemy, as he turned out to be last time, as you remember. I was worried about you and our other friends. Well, Michele asked me if I wanted a huge green hat with a long strange black feather: it was rather absurd, I thought. He didn't seem to recognize me. But, you know, the slave poet is cunning, like the cleverest of foxes in the world. Someone could have thought we were friends. It could have been dangerous for us. So, after a while, he winked at me and said: 'Follow me, Monsieur, please. Behind that wall I have other hats for a gentilhomme *like you.'*

'So you and Michele went away,' I say.

It's clear you don't know Michele at all. There are men that love money more than their mother. Eagerness is a human feeling that is a suit for him, a forma mentis *stronger than all his other senses. 'It seems people like my hats. It would be a pity not to take advantage of this opportunity, wouldn't it?' he said, smiling when we reached the place full of* marvellous *hats behind the wall. There were many hats on a wooden table. Each of them with its tricolour cockade. Apropos of this, Lorenzo, I imagine you noticed the people go round without cockades on their hats here. Another serious historical mistake. Look at mine, please!*

'Yes, it has its big tricolour cockade. As usual, you are right, Professor. But I think that we could leave all things as they are now.'

It's no use insisting with you, Lorenzo. You are pig-headed. All right, this world is yours. Well. I said that Michele wanted to make some money. So I helped him. Several women were attracted by our hats and, I must be honest, I had a good time. Yes! Try to imagine an old gentlewoman quarrelling with a lower-class girl over a dark grey witch's hat. It's true, I swear! And I remember a fat, tall woman forcing a passage through the crowd, then, when she was by our stall, demanding: 'Have you seen my husband? He is short with a red potato-shaped nose and an enormous hat like that.' She pointed to a not particularly handsome brown hat. 'I think he just went across the market.'

Michele said laughing: 'Must you give him a sound beating?'

'No, Monsieur,*' she replied, 'he was drunk and when he is drunk he repeats the same terrible sentence…'*

I doubted whether words could be so terrible and she went on: 'These words are so terrible that I cannot repeat them aloud but, if you want, I can whisper them in your ear.' She put her mouth near my face: 'Long live the king! Death to the Jacobins!'

Later, with a heavy bag full of francs, we went to a place where I would have met an important man for our destiny. I ought to have asked Michele many questions about him and his friend Palandro, who is so close to Robespierre. But people were shouting and there was an incredible confusion of carts, cabs and coaches of various kinds that overwhelmed our thoughts and us. At one point a cattle cart passed by, slow and solemn. Around the cart's sides a macabre line of legs and arms from the bodies of men and women festooned the edge. Fresh blood fell on the road. People witnessing that human mess turned their backs: not from pity or disgust, but out of habit. Terrible, my friend! I'm glad you couldn't see these horrible things. You are so sensitive!

'Like a girl, I know, Professor. I know. It's a problem for me. But please go on. It is very interesting,' I say.

And you haven't heard it all, my friend. Michele finally left me alone in a massive grey walled palace, in a large high-ceilinged room rich with precious furniture. I would have met an English nobleman who lives there incognito, but at that moment he had an important guest. Michele would have returned soon so I should have remained calm. He knew what he was doing. Well, I thought, maybe that's true. Then, in the silence I overheard two men conversing. '…they have seen the medicine of the state corrupted into its poison,' an old man's voice said. Now, I don't want to seem conceited, but if I say I am a cultured man, it's simply true, and when I heard those words, they weren't new to me and I realised that that man certainly knew what he was talking about and I would have liked to shake his hand.

'But who was he?' I ask.

Edmund Burke, a practical and wise man.

'Oh, Edmund Burke. And who was his host, this mysterious English nobleman? Don't speak. I can see him, you know... A curious chap indeed.' I exclaim laughing. 'It's ridiculous: the Scarlet Pimpernel! "Those French seek him everywhere." Ridiculous indeed.'

He is a most educated and elegant man. He is a baronet. Anyway, he is no more ridiculous than Shoe, Suit and Sweat, lad. And I must remark on his pleasant manners. When I managed to meet him, he apologised for not introducing me to his friend; but Edmund Burke had to leave Paris immediately. 'They will execute Louis de Saint-Just tomorrow night. The French are too excited at the moment. It is extremely dangerous for us to do our work in this diabolical place,' he said and declaimed: 'But it is our *job and* our *folk need* our *help.'*

'But do you remember who the Scarlet Pimpernel is?' I ask.

I must remind you that I am much older than you, Lorenzo, and I know all you know and more than you can imagine. He is the principal character in plays and adventure novels by Baroness Emmuska Orczy.

'I apologise, Professor, but...'

*But nothing! Listen to me. He told me frankly who he was:
'My name is Percy Blakeney, for my friends; for the French, I am
the Scarlet Pimpernel.'*

*A man in rags came in and said: 'Not all French are
Jacobins, mon ami.'*

*'Oh, dear Jean, just in time to meet our new friend...
Apropos, I don't remember your name, Sir,' Blakeney said.*

*'I haven't told you yet. I am Egisto Cavallo, the actor-
manager of* The Cavallo Touring Company. *But it seems
odd not to know my name, yet you state that you are my friend.' I
said.*

'Michele is my friend. This is all I need.'

*The Frenchman added: 'I didn't know your name either or
rather, I didn't remember it, but I saw you on stage some days
ago.'*

'What do you think of Henri IV *by Luigi Pirandello?'*

'Marvellous but strange, mon ami. *To be honest, I would
have liked a* pièce *in which monarchist ideas were stronger. That
man is a poor lunatic or, worse, a cunning and dishonest chap.'*

*Sir Blakeney felt the need to explain to me that his friend was
a monarchist, full of energy and fervour, but that nonetheless he
appreciated my anti-revolutionary courage and my talent as actor.
His friend was full of enthusiasm as he described my
performance. But he was Jean-Nicolas Stofflet, the major general
in the Catholic-Royalist Grand Army. He was organizing the
Vendean rebellion against the Republicans. He always had to be
strong; after all he was a leader.*

*Yes, Lorenzo, a leader but also a good person, I think. This
wasn't a problem. What made me feel uneasy was my situation as
a man of the future, my particular historical point of view. The
French Revolution is not negative for me, the world as we know it
is predicated on it as a constitutional element. But we are men of
the future, we can be neither against nor completely for anybody in
this time, or in any time other than our own. But I am an enemy*

of violence in all times, and saving innocent people from the guillotine is a good job, I think. Indeed, my own job in this particular age.

'My job too,' I declare.

It couldn't be differently, dear. And this is the key to solving the ambiguity of Michele's behaviour. We thought he was an enemy and we know he is a friend of Palandro's. And Palandro is close to Robespierre. What is the common thread through this mess? That we are all extraneous to events in this era; that we do not belong. This is the solution that explains the incongruity of our enemies' behaviour, the tendency for them (and for us) to act in ways that are alien to this age and contradictory in themselves.

'So Palandro is doing something to help our imprisoned friends,' I say.

Not simply imprisoned but under a death sentence, Lorenzo. To the guillotine, tonight. Yes, Palandro is our ally in this instance. Probably he and Michele have never been enemies. Who knows? The situation is complex and unclear. It deserves our focussed and constant attention. Anyway, the Scarlet Pimpernel began to explain the plan of action to free our friends. It consists in attacking the Republicans when they are celebrating their cruel guillotine ceremony. 'We will converge from many points on Place de la Révolution, where the guillotine will be set up,' he said. 'My men will be with us, dear Cavallo. Jean with his soldiers will arrive from other corners, and Coralba and her wild women…'

'What! Cora? Wild women?' I exclaim.

'Yes, my sad Romeo: my women will be decisive, as women usually are,' Cora says, laughing.

Cora and Palandro are standing by our bench, gazing calmly at us. Behind them a tall, handsome and elegant man is absorbed in the observation of his white gloves.

It appears that this is a narrators' meeting; each narrator anxious to share his adventures. Paris is always a great maker of stories, a prodigious mother of all sensations, emotions, ideas… Seeing our group around a bench arouses a strong feeling in me. It reminds me of when I was a child with my friends in the courtyard – gathered between benches, trees and bits of scant meadow – close to a bigger and better courtyard that nonetheless was not so magical as ours. Mino, Oscar, Enrico, Tiziano, Daniele, Robertino and Armando: in short, all my friends and I would stand around a bench all afternoon telling stories and living them so intensely that they turned into what we wanted. Adults walking by the courtyard saw only some kids on a bench, not their castles, lakes complete with the monster, Ness, terrible knights and beautiful princesses. It was autumn and the leaf was gold and slow as it fell and touched Oscar's nose. And he shouted, afraid: 'The monster, the monster!' Now, and remarkably this is the same, it seems that Coralba will exclaim: "The monster, the monster." Listen to her:

I found my wild women – as you define them – at the outset of this problem, I mean in the theatre when the gendarmes *arrested our friends. There were three women in the third row. I noticed them during the play, especially Claire, who seemed particularly interested in our performance. She is an actress. Pauline owns a chocolate store and Manon is a bourgeois intellectual and disciple of Rousseau.*

'*Madame,*' Sir Percy Blakeney interjects, 'I think you are speaking about Claire Lacombe, Pauline Léon and Manon Roland. Can it be so?'

Exactly, Pimpernel! I see you are puzzled by this.

'Dear, you display an unreasonable antagonism towards me. Is there a problem?'

These circumstances are the problem, Flower-Maybe-Scarlet. Your political ideas are the problem for me, for my revolutionary conscience. I consider myself a woman of the Revolution. I belong to the Revolutionary Republic of Women.

'Incredible! A *sans-culotte* woman that wants to save people from the guillotine! The world is upside down indeed. And, as to my seeming 'puzzled', I would like to know why *Madame* Roland has become the friend of an extremist like you. It is well-known that she is a member of the Girondist faction.'

I didn't know that monarchist *was a synonym for* impatient. *I was about to tell you what happened to me. Listen and you will know what you want about Manon Roland. Well. As I said, they were there when the* gendarmes *came to arrest us in our theatre. The three women quickly whisked me out of there to a shanty near the place where we had parked our 1958 Beardmore Taxi.*

The shanty was full of silence. It was very poor inside. A big wooden table with no chairs in the middle. A narrow window and a door that was as small as that of a doll's house. The dirty floor and ceiling were rich in cobwebs and insects. It was already evening outside and the solitary candle on the table lit our silent figures in a strange way. Claire and Pauline were in front of me, behind the table. Manon was in a dark corner and I sensed that she didn't want to be there. I couldn't see their faces very well, but heard their heavy breathing after the flight.

That silence seemed replete not only with fear and exhaustion, but a tension between us; a net of contrasts and bonds tightening in the dark that was broken only by the yellow flame.

A strange dialogue began in which Claire spoke, looking only at me. I followed the conversation from the position of their shapes. Pauline was in profile turned towards Claire, and Manon, so sunk in a dark corner, was a black stain communicating with nobody. The geometry of the women's bodies expressed their mood, and I was clearly the problem.

'We'll be safe here, Claire. But it is preposterous to take risks for her, a royalist, simply because she is an actress like you,' said Pauline in the voice of someone who is always angry with the world, and as if she were answering a question.

'If you understood the theatre a little, you wouldn't say such a foolish thing. That comedy concerns neither monarchy nor revolution, it is the story of a crazy or cunning man who wants to take revenge on his rival in love,' Claire said, still looking at me, her voice calm and pleasant. Then she said to me: 'Isn't it true, dear? I don't know your name.'

'Coralba,' I said, 'but I prefer Cora. And yes, that is true of Pirandello's comedy. And your name, please?'

At this point Manon spoke from behind the others, but she seemed to address someone seen only by her: 'It is always difficult for me to understand them when they speak, because there is something instinctive that motivates them, not reason. Even this actress belongs to the same sort of simple-minded people. But there is Olympe de Gouges to save.'

'But who is she speaking about?' I asked Claire.

'Who are you speaking about, dear?'

'The lady behind you, obviously.'

'She wasn't speaking, dear. When she is with us she considers us like pupils unworthy of praise. But, I think I should introduce us to her. I am Claire Lacombe, in front of me Pauline Léon and behind me Manon Roland, who spoke, according to you, a moment ago. Pauline and I founded the Society of Revolutionary Republican Women. We are sans-culottes. Manon, however, is a member of the Girondist faction, a disciple of Rousseau, and an intellectual, not uneducated like us...'

'My dear Cora,' interjects the professor, 'you have already given us all this information about the women, and we obviously know everything about Pirandello's comedy. I must suggest that you do not imitate Lorenzo in his tendency to repeat the same information continually.'

I will try. But listen to what happened, please. Suddenly a beam of electric light from an invisible source appeared, illuminating a corner of the room. Two men in Twenty-first Century work clothes came in carrying a big poster of Rousseau

97

– portrayed as an elegant and good-looking man – and placed it against the wall before leaving through an invisible door. From Rousseau's image came a pleasant voice: 'Childhood is the sleep of reason.'

Apropos of these men and their talking poster, Dear Creator, you could have chosen a better narrative *solution. Still, at least your version of Rousseau censured your strange mind-set, I mean, of course, your Peter Pan Complex, and your truly bizarre world.*

'No comment,' I say, snorting. 'My dear audience in the wall understands all this very well. After all, don't I endlessly repeat myself, as the professor pointed out?'

'But I like the talking poster. It reminds me of a Woody Allen film-device. It's a cheerful solution,' declares Palandro, laughing.

'I don't know who Woody Allen is, Palandro. But I think that Rousseau wasn't so elegant as you made out, dear Cora,' Sir Percy Blakeney affirms, laughing in his turn.

'I will say only a word on this matter: perhaps there are times when mankind needs to sleep, putting aside his terrible Reason,' says the professor, seriously.

All this is very interesting, dear friends, but do allow me to finish my story. Well. As I said, the picture of Rousseau spoke only to its disciple, Manon – I could also hear and see him. The other two women could neither hear nor see the poster, nor could they hear Manon. And neither Manon nor the image of her Master seemed to hear or see me. We were in a state of incommunicability. I think that is the right word. Or better, we were only partly able to communicate, each of us variously secluded or excluded by the others' behaviour. Does my explanation seem correct, Professor?

Egisto Cavallo nods imperceptibly.

Maybe the principal problem wasn't my being among them as I'd first thought.

'The education of women,' declaimed the poster in a stentorian voice, 'should always be relative to that of men.'

It's remarkable how things can turn on one right (or wrong) word. I paid so much attention to explaining what I meant by incommunicability *because I know how situations can change when there is too much communication. Listen to what happened next!*

Pauline turned like a Fury: 'What is that? Someone is speaking foolishness and I can't see him.'

But the picture, imperturbable, went on with its speech. 'To please, to be useful to us, to make us love and esteem them, to educate us when young, to take care of us when grown up, to advise, to console us, to render our lives easy and agreeable...'

'Marvellous!' Claire said with an ironic tone, 'I have always dreamed of being a man's slave. But who and where is this stupid man?'

'It is not a man. It is only a thing,' I said timidly.

'Yes,' said Manon, 'a thing, or rather an image of a great man.'

'You may call him great, if you want, but he is really stupid, dear,' barked Pauline, turning to Manon.

Do you know The Chioggia Scuffles *by Carlo Goldoni? Well. There was a general uproar reminiscent of the play, in which that parody of Rousseau spoke again, and everyone could hear: 'These are the duties of women at all times, and what they should be taught in their infancy.'*

'Take that dammed thing away!' shouted Pauline, who could now see the poster.

As if it were an order that summoned them, the two men reappeared and took away the image of the philosopher.

'You shouldn't have done that!' Manon shouted, falling on Pauline's neck.

Claire and I jumped into the brawl to help Pauline. Everyone against the Girondist. It was unsporting behaviour, but this is normal in political matters. I chose what is usual for me: to be an

99

extremist in all things, because I can only achieve anything significant in my life in that way. I am a Montagnarde!

And in any case it was amusing to join in.

It was amusing, but noisy. So the *gendarmes* had arrested the four careless women. This is me, the creator, speaking, and I am addressing you directly, as an actor does when he goes to the edge of the stage to tell something to those stalls. Palandro quivers with impatience to give us his account, but it is my work to describe the details of how the scuffle ended, and then to introduce him and his adventure.

Well. An old carpenter wanted to put his tools away in that shanty, so he heard the women shouting and crying and moaning. He decided to call the *gendarmes*. Soon after Cora, Claire, Pauline and Manon were sitting on the floor. The battle was over. A new silence wrapped their hot faces and ruffled hair. The effort seemed to have changed their feelings for each other. It was not love exactly, but something had changed between them. Previously their bond had been based only on a common aim: to save their friends from the guillotine. More precisely to save Olympe de Gouges, who, although she was a Girondist, spoke and wrote for all female citizens when she wrote: "Woman is born free and lives equal to man in her rights." And she would be guillotined, if they didn't manage to help her.

In spite of her recent political persuasion, Cora was concerned only of her friends and their safety. When the *gendarmes* arrived and arrested them, she hardly noticed the danger to herself. But first let us hear from Palandro; his account of meeting Cora and what happened after.

It is a huge building made of glass and steel. Robespierre behaved normally, but nothing was strange for him. His office is in there full of normal, for this period, furniture. The authorities brought Cora and her friends there. At the time, I was looking through the wide window that overlooks the Place de la Révolution. Some men were preparing the guillotine, and a discussion began on this matter.

'Do you want your executioner to guillotine Olympe de Gouges this evening?' demanded Pauline Léon.

Robespierre remained calm, like a seraphic priest and his voice was not masculine; his small, delicate hands were on the top of the writing desk where he sat. There was something mellifluous about his demeanour... No! I refuse to continue. I must declare my disagreement with this depiction of Robespierre. I decline to see him in this way, through Lorenzo's eyes. Therefore I will stop describing the person, who is a friend of mine.

'I didn't realize I had made him so... unpleasant,' I say carefully. 'I don't really know anything about him.'

Self-criticism is always a laudable thing. As I said, I will avoid speaking about my friend's appearance or his voice. I will focus my attention on his words. And apropos of this, listen to how he answered Pauline's question.

'Citoyenne Léon, I invite you to reflect on your situation. And I am not referring to the ludicrous reason that led you here, but to your recent behaviour in general; and not only yours,' said the Incorruptible, regarding the group of enragés.

'Citoyen Robespierre, my friend, as usual, speaks in all sincerity forgetting the political suitability of the current moment,' Claire Lacombe interjected. 'But she is a truly honest woman and a good revolutionary, as you know. Friendship is the feeling compelling her to behave in such an awkward manner. Please accept my apologies for her. As concerns our recent offence, it was only a lively discussion about our divergence of views.'

'I think the divergence of views is the soul of our Revolution,' declared Manon Roland, smiling at him, 'the breeding-ground of great ideas. It would be ridiculous if you, Citoyen Président, *condemned us for this.'*

'President of what?' I ask.

Of the Convention, Lorenzo. But listen. During this conversation, Cora had been glaring at me with great hostility.

'It is obvious, Palandro, that I didn't know the truth then. I thought of imitating that young Girondist... that Charlotte... who someone here knows very well,' Cora replies with a mocking smile at me.

I can't understand how she came to know of it. I'm afraid that I blushed in shame.

'Don't be silly, Lorenzo,' exclaims Sir Percy Blakeney. 'You are a man. There's no need to have any other consideration. You are only a man. Don't worry!'

It is not important. Charlotte Corday is another person we must save tonight, but going back to my story about Cora, I beckoned her to me. The office is large and I led her to a corner by the window. Before I could say anything, she began calling me such names, whispering with a terrible red face, that I thought she might beat me, or worse. I understood her reasons. But my friendship for Robespierre doesn't mean that I agree with him about his determination to put my friends to death. I tried to convince him that it was a terrible mistake to execute innocent actors, but it was impossible. He is as hard as stone and my insistence on it could have pushed him to consider me a bad revolutionary, a possible traitor to our Revolution.

'Our? I thought it was only Cora that doesn't know when to stop,' the professor says.

But maybe my imagination knows when to stop; everything around me crumbles into a familiar white gash... an enormous hungry mouth engulfing me...

9

IF I THINK

You need not leave your room. Remain sitting at your table and listen. You need not even listen, simply wait, just learn to become quiet and still, and solitary. The world will freely offer itself to you to be unmasked. It has no choice; it will roll in ecstasy at your feet.

Franz Kafka,
Zurau Aphorisms

awake – that is if remaining still for a long time can be called sleeping, as if you were unconscious but with eyes wide-open – and I see the French window. I look through it: no Cora, no Professor, no Palandro, no Shoe, Suit and Sweat, no Molière, no Olympe de Gouges or Robespierre, no Fitzgerald and Zelda, neither the Enemy nor the Bard... no Charlotte (everything has vanished); not those deceptive (and real) swallows you have come to know very well. There are only normal (yet also deceptive) trees, cars, and common people opening their umbrellas because it's starting to rain, and my collected poems, which are real in this reality too. There is a piece of paper among its pages: a message from my wife? *Important! Write to Twm Thomas. Don't forget! Silvana.* But I can't remember why I am supposed to be doing this or who Twm Thomas is. I don't really care. I'm too tired to remember anything or anyone.

What is the matter with me? In the last few days I keep falling into a strange and sudden sleep; in the middle of a thought or while I'm trying to relax. And everything changes, the entire world in my mind: I am aboard that wrecked Beardmore or in the midst of a female quarrel during the French Revolution. It was a meaningless story that I didn't write, but lived with the intensity of a realistic and incredible dream. Maybe I'm hallucinating. No, rather, it was an alternate reality that steadily took the place of the common one, inside me... Let me clarify one point in this chaos at least.

I have been shut up in my small flat for a week. The reason? I don't know. I live on the ninth floor, the top floor in a light blue block of flats on a large avenue. I am watching everything collapse from up here. I could

105

say the entire planet. I see something rising to the surface of this imaginary grey morning lake: a hat, a doll's head, a yellow baby-doll, a set of crystal glasses, and a set of crystal noises emanate from the deep water that surrounds my castle. And I also hear…

On the eighth floor a woman and her husband quarrel every day. They burst my eardrums every day. Yesterday they quarrelled about "Abelardo". They spoke about the "third floor" and "Mehmed II" and "a state of siege" and "he died, poor chap" and "Constantinople"… I think they are history teachers and Abelardo is a flat owner. I don't know my neighbours. I remember an incomplete list of names and a gallery of faces full of blanks, and I am not able to match them rightly. Abelardo. He could be that short man with a prominent belly and a mouth full of teeth and saliva, or that slim, tall, elegant old gentleman, who always wears a black bowler hat… Who knows?

Maybe I am only looking for a pretext to admit to defeat with humanity. But Teresa, the caretaker, who is looking after me while my wife is away on a school trip, is an ambassador of peace for humankind and brings me some decent food and a few blameless words about the life of our block of flats. She is coming as usual. It is half past eleven in the morning.

'Remain sitting at your table and listen,' she says.

'Do you like Kafka, Teresa?'

'No. But I tried to read him because my son loves his books. Why?' she answers, surprisingly.

'It's not important. What have you brought me, today?'

She puts her two heavy carrier bags on the table in the dining room, one full of fruit and vegetables and the other with two food containers and a bottle of beer. She prepares meals for me twice a day, every day, and always brings them at half past eleven in the morning and at seven o'clock in the evening.

'Would you like some pasta salad and some good hot stew?' she asks, smiling.

'Oh yes. This is very important, not only for my stomach.'

The dialogue between us rattles through the small flat. I am sitting at my desk in front of the French window and the large balcony, facing west towards the Alps, in my odd bedroom that is full of study furniture. She is on the other side of the apartment, in the dining room, which has a small kitchen to the right and another large balcony toward the east and the hills, on the left. In the middle there is a very small entrance: if you come in through the front door, you see two doors: one leads to a box-room, the other to a bathroom. This isn't an ordinary flat in my mind; it is Jonah's whale, or a silver rocket protecting me, even a new and comfortable womb from which I could be born again, perhaps.

'Would you like a cup of coffee, Teresa?' I ask, joining her at the table.

'Yes, please. You are always very kind, Lorenzo.'

'Please, sit down. I'll put these things in the kitchen and make some coffee.'

Now the woman is sitting at the table in the dining room. Her huge, pleasant body is like a marshmallow covered with a cheerful and comical overall. It settles onto that poor chair.

'*Grazie*,' Teresa says, receiving the coffee from my hands. 'How long have you been in this flat without going out?'

'Almost one week.'

'But do you have to stay indoors? This way of living is bad for your health, dear Lorenzo. You look pale.'

'It's too complicated to explain, and too long. Don't worry about me, Teresa. I like this situation. It's strange, I know, but I like it.'

While I am thinking that in fact I don't like it that much, some words surface in my memory: "March 30th, 2003 – Suicide Bombing in Netanya, Israel, wounded 38 people, only the bomber was killed". Strange, I began this separation from the world on the same day. It is obviously pure coincidence. It is the umpteenth malevolent emanation in the world, not even the most serious evil, but it was part of what pushed me to remain in this simultaneously comfortable and uncomfortable corner. The world is false like a bad film, but kills and destroys.

'Would you be interested in what happened yesterday in the cellars? Well, Mr. Ditone quarrelled with the butcher. They were screaming about the flooding of Ditone's cellar. It seems the water came from the butcher's cellar. It's a mess that...'

'I heard Abelardo is dead,' I interrupt her.

'Abelardo?'

'Yes, Abelardo, the flat owner on the third floor.'

'I know all the people that live here very well, as any good caretaker does, and I can say I have never heard of Abelardo.'

Contrary to what Teresa perhaps believes, it is possible that Mehmed II the Conqueror is laying siege to our block of flats... *if* I think.

NOTES

Chapter 3:

Referring to characters as Lorenzo's "own blood" (p. 31) is an allusion to *Le Furie* (*The Furies*) by Guido Piovene (1907-1974). Piovene was born in Vicenza; a novelist, journalist, and special correspondent, he wrote metaphysical, fantastic literature.

References to Baudrillard (pp. 32-34) are free adaptions from an article in *Le Monde*, 02.11.2001 and an interview with him in *Der Spiegel*, no.3, 2002.

Chapter 4:

Zelda's speech about being a buttercup (p. 41) is freely adapted from a sentence Daisy said in Chapter 1 of *The Great Gatsby*: '...I'm glad it's a girl. And I hope she'll be a fool – that's the best thing a girl can be in this world, a beautiful little fool', which was in turn freely adapted by Fitzgerald from a sentence Zelda often repeated.

Fitzgerald made the statement about not knowing whether he and Zelda were characters in one of his books (p.44) in Spring 1933 at the La Paix estate on the outskirts of Baltimore.

Chapter 7:

(p. 82) Lecture by Augusto Romano for a seminar in Catania on 13th May 2001: *The Land that Does Not Exist: Nostalgia for the Origins and Feelings of the World.*

Chapter 8:

'…they have seen the medicine of the state corrupted into its poison,' (p. 92) is from *Reflections on the Revolution in France*, Edmund Burke, 1790.

The reference to the Scarlet Pimpernel being sought for everywhere by the French (p. 92) is an allusion to 'The Scarlet Pimpernel's poem' in the play, *The Scarlet Pimpernel*, Baroness Orczy, 1905.

Free references to: *Deviant Women of the French Revolution* by Lisa Beckstrand, 2009. (pp. 94-96)

'Childhood is the sleep of reason.' (p. 98) is from *Émile or On Education*, Rousseau, 1762.

Chapter 9:

Newspaper titles (p. 108) from articles on the web.

AUTHOR BIOGRAPHY

ANDREA BIANCHI is a translator from English to Italian and from Italian to English. Together with his wife, Silvana, he has translated some of the most important voices of Welsh literature such as Dannie Abse, Myrddin ap Dafydd, Tony Curtis, Menna Elfyn, Harri Pritchard Jones, Gwyneth Lewis, Iwan Llwyd, Robert Minhinnick, Caradog Prichard, Wiliam Owen Roberts, R.S.Thomas and others, besides conceiving the series: *Minorities not Minority: a Window on Italian Cultures* published by Cinnamon Press.

Andrea is a poet in Italian and a prose writer in English. His first collection of translated poems, *A Corridor of Rain*, was published by Cinnamon Press in 2011. *Fellinesque* is his first novella. He lives in Turin.